Gift of Story

Gift of Story

A Faerie's Tale for Childish Grown-ups

Carmen M Clark

authorHOUSE®

AuthorHouse™
1663 Liberty Drive
Bloomington, IN 47403
www.authorhouse.com
Phone: 1 (800) 839-8640

Published by AuthorHouse   03/04/2015

ISBN: 978-1-4918-1872-5 (sc)
ISBN: 978-1-4918-1870-1 (hc)
ISBN: 978-1-4918-1869-5 (e)

Library of Congress Control Number: 2013917512

Print information available on the last page.

Dedications

To Aaron (my cutie-pie), to Maria (my free-spirited faerie), and to Ivan (my leprechaun), the three magical loves of my life

And to every single person who perseveres in making his or her dream a reality and the people who never stop cheering others on

Acknowledgements

Firstly, I would like to thank my mother, Maria Morris.
I thank my husband, who is my infinite strength.
I thank Stephanie Triolo, Becky Jacobs, and Reyna Lingamann, three
kick-ass women whose support helped make this book happen.
Thank you to Veronica Flinn, whose cover
art gave my story a beautiful image.
Thank you to Wei Hwu for capturing such a lovely photograph of me.
Thank you to everyone who pledged on Kickstarter, who helped
me pick out an author photograph, who was excited to hear
about this book, who had a kind word, a high-five, or a hug.

Cover art: Veronica Flinn, www.veronicaflinn.com
Author photograph: Wei Hwu, www.thetiniestbird.com

"Why don't they show themselves? Damn faeries," said Maggie O'Malley. She was sick of Suzy, from two houses over, being so bossy, and tired of Bobby, from down the street, who was in trouble again. His parents knew Maggie was the mastermind; she was the one who convinced him to set a frog on Ms. Jenkins's chair, but he was in trouble nonetheless. They hoped that he would get fed up with being punished and therefore tire of playing with Maggie.

Which is why Maggie was by herself, looking for faeries. She knew they existed; she knew it like she knew green was green, and up was up, and round was round. There were some things that just were, and one of them was the existence of faeries. Her patience, however, was being tested since she could not find a single trace. Each blade of grass went under her magnifying glass, the flowers gently combed, and the garden beds inspected, but nothing. Thoroughly frustrated, and with the sun beginning to set, she decided it was time to call it quits. In a show of stubbornness and independence rare for a nine-year-old, Maggie had rummaged through the garage until she'd found the old camping tent and set it up in the yard. She looked at it now with a mixture of excitement and perhaps a bit of anxiety. Their acres of land were not fully fenced, and she'd heard the coyotes howl in the distance. Calculating in her mind, she determined it to be only fifty yards from the back door of the house and then reminded herself that her father, Robert, had insisted on giving her one of the walkie-talkies. If a coyote came too close or if the faeries were to try to abduct her, she had her father at the press of a button. Giving the garden, with its fruit trees, vegetables, and flowers of every shape and size, one last glance, she climbed into the tent, zipping it up behind her.

Robert and his daughter both had the same thick, dark brown hair, so dark it was almost black, and the same startling blue eyes. Maggie shared the light complexion of her father, and a sprinkle of freckles across her nose made her lovelier. Maggie's mother, Matilda, had green eyes, and her skin a darker tone, but her long hair was just as dark as that of her husband and daughter.

Maggie wore her hair down, always somewhat messy and always somewhat in her eyes. After it became clear Maggie would not take care of her clothes when she was out romping around, Matilda bought an army of blue jeans and a rainbow of plain T-shirts for Maggie to play in, leaving a couple of nice outfits for when they went to events. On these special occasions, the littlest O'Malley was never too thrilled to have her jeans taken away, a battle Matilda would have to gear up for.

Lying in her sleeping bag, Maggie again tried to decide what faeries might actually look like. Were they the faeries from the flower books? With wings and pastel colors? Or were they more human, like the ones in her mother's stories? The saccharine-sweet faeries bored her, but the more human ones seemed overly sinister. They were real to her when Matilda told her stories, these faeries that did not fly so much as appear and disappear. These faeries that were sometimes noble and other times terrifying excited Maggie, and as she zoomed her flashlight across the ceiling of the tent, she pretended they were out there, in the dark, doing something fun and dangerous.

As it turns out, the O'Malley's yard was being occupied by a faerie. Had Maggie pointed her flashlight a few yards to the left and down behind the apple tree, she would have seen Missy Wendolyn Brightwing, small even for a faerie, standing not more than nine inches tall. Her wings, when she chose to show them, were gold like her hair, with oranges and yellows woven finely through. Maggie would have been surprised to find that faeries are a little of everything she'd seen or heard: humanoid, but more brilliant in color than those in her faerie flower books. They were enchanting, eccentric, frightening, and lovely. Had Maggie been allowed to wander through the meadow in the back of their ten acres, she would have been very close to one of the portals to Faerie. It didn't look like much; actually, it looked like nothing at all because the hole at the base of a giant redwood to a human would look just like that: a hole at the base of a giant redwood. Maggie, though, was not allowed to wander the back acres of the O'Malley property, at least not without an adult. It was rare to have a parent Not Busy, and if they were Not Busy, then usually they were Doing Something Else, which they would insist was different from being Busy.

Missy Wendolyn Brightwing was wondering how she could possibly finish her job with this horrible obtrusion. She studied the tent and reassured herself that it was not a monster. She'd seen the little girl walk in and out of it; surely it was not a monster.

The little girl intrigued Wendolyn. There was something familiar about her; she could sense it. Her body reverberated with a twang. Tossing her bright gold hair out of the way, she decided she'd have to wait until the little girl fell asleep to finish her task.

Wendolyn's chief job was to gather pollen of various kinds to make faerie coins, and the sort she needed at the moment was much too close to the humans for her taste. It was the only garden with the best varieties of flowers—not just the average roses, jasmine, daisies, and black-eyed Susans but also tulips and lilies of every type, wisteria dripped from fences, bushes of lavender, both English and French, daffodils and crocus, iris and flowering maples. Wendolyn loved this garden and would often visit just to eat a few raspberries or to pick a lemon. She would only come at night, when the humans were in their beds, but tonight the little girl was out at night, or inside what seemed to be a portable bedroom. This was the closest she'd ever gotten to a human before, and it made her nervous.

All faeries avoided humans unless, of course, they were bored. Faeries can have a wicked sense of humor, and humans—with their slow thinking and flair for the dramatic—were wonderful playthings for the bored faerie. This is not to say that faeries do not have human friends; on the contrary, especially in older countries, faeries have great human friends, and those friends are very happy about the alliance. Faeries are fiercely loyal and vicious fighters, a plus for humans in trouble.

"You expect me to believe that?" I ask. What Juniper and I have is no friendship; it is more a master-and-servant dynamic.

She looks at me like I'm subhuman. "Of course," she says and goes on brushing her perfectly silky, brick-red hair.

Juniper is ethereal, but then, she is a faerie. She doesn't have wings, or if she does, they are hidden. I kind of don't want to see them; it seems a little too fantastical, and I'm not ready for that. She looks human, I mean, she's roughly my height and has two arms and legs and one head, but there is something magnetizing about her. People stare at her when we walk down the street together. She has delicate features, is graceful in action, and her clothes are a mix of lace, leather, and every color in the rainbow. Need a purple shirt or a blue skirt? Her style is impeccable. Right now, she's wearing tight leather pants and an avocado-green tunic shirt with a thick black belt. With her red hair wildly framing her face, I'm telling you, she looks like a rock goddess.

I watch her, her fingers combing through the long strands, and a pang courses through my body. She is like all the pretty girls, a total bitch. I want to brush her off, but then she pulls me in. Is it magic? Curiosity? I've never met a faerie before. She is, but isn't, what I'd expect. Not that I'm making any sense. Maybe it's the vodka; we've run out of mixer, and I've been sipping it straight for half an hour. Juniper could drink me under the table; I have to be careful around her. To my one, she has three and doesn't show it.

"Hi? Hello? Where did you go, silly Charlotte?" Juniper waves her hand in front of my face, snapping me out of my thoughts.

"I want to go out. Let's go somewhere, one of those dance clubs," she says.

"Are you kidding?" I ask. "I hate dance clubs. They play horrible music, and everyone's gyrating, and lets face it, straight-up dry humping. And it always smells like kitty litter and ass."

Juniper looks at me puzzled. "I don't know that."

"Kitty litter?"

"No, the other, dry …"

"Humping, you know, it's like, uh, having sex but with your clothes on, so you're not actually Doing It?"

Juniper looks at me, horrified. "That sounds stupid. And uncomfortable."

I sigh. "It is."

Juniper jumps up and claps her hands once as if to command attention. "We are going, and we will watch these stupid humans do this thing, and it will be fun." She turns to me. "They will have this vodka, right?"

I snort; of course she thinks of alcohol. "Can you at least leave me alone for an hour? I'm writing this for you after all."

She actually has the temerity to stomp into my room and slam my door.

Just as I'm hunkering down to get some writing done, the telephone rings. Caller ID says it's my sister. Okay. I'll answer, talk for ten minutes, and then get back to writing. Yeah, fucking right. I can never go less than half an hour with Joan, and I don't even remember what we talk about.

"He-he-ey. What's-su-up?" I say into the phone.

Joan sighs a long, I'm-calling-to-check-in-on-you-for-Mom type of sigh.

"Hi, Char. How's it going?"

I look at my bedroom door and picture Juniper trying on my makeup.

"W-well, it's b-bbeen interesting. I ha-aave a new r-rr-oom mate."

"Oh? Well, that's good." Joan is genuinely surprised.

Ah-ha, derailed her. "You didn't tell me you were getting a roommate."

Thinking of that night at Flannigan's, I answer, "I-i-it was un-unexpected."

"I talked to Mom last night—and before you cut me off—you know how she worries. Seriously, I tell her you're fine, but, well, you know her. She thinks you hole yourself up and don't get out enough."

It's my turn to sigh. "I-I-I know."

"But this'll cheer her up. Can I tell her details? Can I *get* details?"

What to tell her? That she's a faerie that suckered me into writing a novel for her and has completely taken over my life?

"Sh-she's a new f-friend, l-l-likes my music b-but doesn't cl-cl-clean up."

"That's it?" I can tell Joan is miffed. I usually tell her everything.

"F-f-for now."

The conversation meanders the way it always does: we laugh, we fight a little, and then after another twenty minutes, we hang up after love yas and g'byes.

Do you notice something? Yeah. Like the *King's Speech* has nothing on me because I can't get over it, unless I'm talking to Juniper. I'm clear as a bell with her, and it's nice to have my words come out so easily. My mom worries because she thinks it's the stutter that makes me unsocial; she worries that I won't find someone to marry and have her grandkids. Maybe that's true. Honestly, I haven't figured it out.

Of course, I was expecting Juniper to be eavesdropping on me, and sure enough, as soon as I click off, she comes in.

"Who was that?"

"None of your business." I turn to get my hat and coat from the coat stand.

"Tell me!"

Ugh. "It was my sister, Joan."

Juniper heads for the shelf where pictures of my family sit in various frames.

"She's pretty."

"Yes. My brother is the funny one, and I'm the smart one."

Juniper raises her eyebrow. "If you're the smart one, these two must be seriously mentally challenged."

"So funny I forgot to laugh."

I walk over to the pictures. There is one of the three of us smiling, arms around each other. It was taken right before I left for the Big City, at the last family function of the summer.

"Joan is smart too, and so is Gilly, but that's how Dad categorized us. That way he knew how to 'deal' with us … he's not much for words or affection. I think it has been harder on Joan than me."

I walk to the door, ready to open it.

"I never had siblings."

I turn to her. "How lonely for you," I reply.

"Well, *my* parents were great, so fun and kind. I don't remember much except it was fun."

"But you faeries all live together, so you had friends, right?"

"Oh, well, yes. I didn't … I had a special situation when I was young."

"Really?" I ask. Despite myself, I'm always interested.

But she changes the topic. "We eat, then we go to the dance club. But not before I pick something out for you to wear. Yes?" she asks but really kind of tells me.

I sigh. "Yeah, sure, whatever." Never mind that I have to get up in the morning to go to work.

M issy Wendolyn pulled back her hair from her eyes and began to fix a hole in her stockings.

She sang softly to herself to help the time go by. A song passed down through generations and roughly twenty-three verses long. With the chorus repeated between each verse, the song lasted a good two hours in human time, which, for a faerie, was no time at all.

After the first couple of verses, she felt peacefulness ebbing from the little girl, guessing that the child had fallen into a deep sleep. Stealthily, Wendolyn made her way to the flowers. Again, as she neared the tent, her body began to reverberate, and she knew there was something different about this child.

Picking the pollen for the coins was not easy, and Missy Wendolyn spent years apprenticing under Master Lightleaf. Wendolyn was a smart faerie; she learned quickly and could memorize spells after one look. She was young for her job but had shown such promise that Master Lightleaf himself taught her. He rarely did that before retiring, but he knew she was a gifted student and deserved his time. She shrunk down small enough to fit into the flowers and gently did her job, all the while thinking of the girl.

The flowers were not far from where the girl slept, so Wendolyn could still feel the odd tingles. She wished she had someone to talk it over with, to share it, because she'd never experienced such a thing. In the old country, so she'd been told, faeries and humans had mingled regularly; there were many half-breeds. She herself had never met one but figured she'd feel the same tingles that she felt right now. Not that she herself looked much different from humans but they were just so … non-magical. There was intrigue about humans for sure, but since her people had come to this country, they'd made a clear point to stay away from them. Humans had the tendency to make situations very complicated.

What if, though, that there had been a tryst betwixt human and faerie? Was this child the product of passionate faerie/human relations? Suddenly realizing she had almost killed the flower by extracting too much pollen, she cursed herself and put her questions aside. They would have to wait for now she had to focus on the task at hand.

Maggie opened her eyes to the early morning sun making the tent glow. If she slit her eyes, she could pretend she wasn't in a tent at all but in an ethereal vortex.

"What's that?" I ask Juniper.

"It's what we call the In-Between," she answers. Like I would understand that?

"Well, what does that mean?" I ask.

"The part you have to travel through to get to Faerie from here or to get here from there." She answers.

Okay.

As Maggie lay, slowly waking up, she tried to remember a dream she had, but it was vague and elusive, and soon she began to wonder if she'd had it at all. Something about gold … what was it?

Shuffling into the house, she met with her parents in the kitchen. As far as parents go, Maggie thought hers were pretty cool, though sometimes a bit too—well—cool. She sometimes wished they weren't, just so she could rebel a little more. This didn't mean she didn't get into trouble; Maggie was the kind of kid that got in trouble a lot, but usually by teachers or other people's parents. She was the kind of girl no one seemed to relate to, no one except her parents.

"Maggie, how was last night?" asked her father after he gave her a big hug.

"I didn't see any faeries, if that's what you mean."

Her mother looked as disappointed as she, and this was one of the many reasons Maggie loved her mother. It was Matilda's stories that inspired Maggie's own imagination. Her mother had a way of pulling you into her stories so that they seemed real; the people or faeries were real, as real as she was sitting there with her parents.

"Well, maybe tonight you'll see something. Would you like to sleep out there again? With some company?" her mother asked.

Maggie sat and thought about this while her father scooped oatmeal into a bowl. Would she like her mother outside? It was nice to be alone, and now that she'd done it once, she felt she could do it the rest of the summer. On the other hand, lying in the tent and falling asleep to her mother's stories sounded heavenly.

"Does that mean I'd get a story?" asked Maggie.

Matilda laughed her catching laugh and replied that of course she would tell Maggie a story.

Maggie grew up with stories. Matilda was the storyteller. Some of what she told was history: hers and Robert's. Maggie grew up knowing that Robert and Matilda came from the same part of Ireland, or so they'd been told. In a rare case of coincidence, they'd been orphaned shortly after arriving, but neither remembered Ireland or even the trip over; both had been very young.

They met in grade school and became lifelong friends, an attraction no person could break. People tried. Girls would slyly try to cage Robert while the boys would spend money on pretty things for Matilda. Robert, however, was impossible to corner for any girl but Matilda, much to the vexation of many pretty girls who spent hours lamenting over him.

Matilda cared nothing for pretty things except for the flowers Robert would pick for her. Had those poor boys only realized they never had a chance, they'd have been able to spend their money a little more wisely. Matilda's aunt and the nice family who took Robert in both weren't surprised; actually it seemed as though they too had been lifelong friends. This was very romantic to Maggie, and often she would make up having her own friend. Suzy and Bobby were fine in a pinch, but there wasn't anyone Maggie felt so attached to. Often, she was quite lonely. She would listen to her mother tell of summers spent with all of them—Matilda, Aunt Lily, Robert, and his folks—vacationing by a lake little populated by people. Hours of festive dinners at each other's houses, birthdays, and other holidays spent together. It wasn't like that now. Neither Matilda nor Robert had many friends; they had people who wanted very badly to be their friends, but no one they especially clicked with, much like their daughter. So usually it was just the three of them—Robert, Matilda, and Maggie—working in the yard or fixing the house or taking nice long bicycle rides.

Matilda grew to be a lovely woman with a laugh that shook one to the core, making all men wish very much it'd been they who'd made her laugh. Robert had grown as handsome as any movie star; he was quick with his wit, and while the men envied him for his girlfriend, the women all wished they were in Matilda's place. It was no surprise when they married, crushing any last hopes of the girls—now women, still pining after Robert—and dashing the fantasies of the grown men who still bought Matilda silly things.

This is when the story got sad, and Maggie would sometimes ask to end the story with her parents' wedding. But sometimes she'd want to hear the sad part and ask her mother to go on. After their nuptials, they moved in with Aunt Lily, and shortly thereafter, she died. It was as if she'd held on to see that Matilda was taken care of before she left this world. Everyone she loved surrounded her bedside when she took her last breath. It was a hard blow to Matilda, who hadn't known any other relation. It turned into a triple tragedy when shortly thereafter came the death of Robert's adopted parents. It seemed after Lily's death, they became reclusive and fearful of life. Robert and Matilda tried to get them to move in with them, but they turned further and further into themselves, eventually wasting away. As Matilda and Robert made sad plans for burials, it struck them how old Robert's parents looked in death. Wrinkles creased the faces of a couple that had seemed almost timeless.

The pain of losing their only family was diminished when Matilda realized she was in a delicate state, and the flurry of getting the house ready for a baby consumed both her and Robert. They named Maggie after Robert's adopted mother and used Lily as her middle name in honor of Matilda's auntie. What had been the old crone's room was stripped of antiques and filled with a crib, books, pillows, and stuffed animals.

The house that Lily Brightwater left to Matilda sat on the edge of town. She had taken such good care of it that everyone in the town was perplexed when, after her passing, the porch began to sag a little, the shutters hung askew, paint didn't look so bright or fresh, and the stairs creaked. Fixing the old house was a favorite of all three O'Malleys, the littlest in charge of painting while Robert and Matilda did the harder things. When they weren't fixing the house, they were gardening, and when they weren't gardening, they would go bicycle riding. Even on very cold days, one could see the family hop on their two wheels and ride away for hours. This suited Maggie just fine as it gave her a sense of independence. She was smart enough to realize it would not be prudent to ride away from her parents, which was an enormous relief to the O'Malleys; once Maggie got an idea in her head, she rarely backed away from it.

"You write like you have a broom up your arse," she says to me.

I look at her disbelieving. Well, that's what I'm going for at any rate.

"I think I've done a fine job at describing this little family."

"You know, Maggie was a big troublemaker," says Juniper, taking a sip of raspberry vodka.

"And I haven't made that clear with Bobby getting in trouble because of her?" I argue. This damn faerie keeps drinking my liquor and arguing over everything. I think I might be reaching my breaking point.

"No, you haven't. Maggie has a terrible swearing problem."

"You mean had? Maggie *had*." I interrupt.

"Yes, yes, *had*. Stop correcting me. She was a very spirited young thing."

I roll my eyes and sigh. "Get me another drink," I say.

As she saunters through the doorway into the kitchen, I survey the mess. My ordinarily clean home has turned into a hovel.

My tiny apartment holds shelves with records, books, CDs, and even cassette tapes. Remember those? Real mixes where you had to pause the tape at the right moment and queue up the next song exactly? I've kept every single one I've ever received.

On top of the shelves are wide ranges of knickknacks, from things I've found at various flea markets to art projects to family photos. Everything usually has a place. There is a spot for everything I own, but since Juniper has barged into my life, my organization has gone to shit. CDs never put back in place, laundry gets stacked up, and the couch has become a bed, which means disheveled blankets. Ugh.

My plants, however, have never looked happier. Like students in a yoga class, they stretch their leaves as if trying to touch all four walls.

Juniper lazily hands me my drink and goes back to looking at some book. Henry Miller? Yep, she's pulled out *Tropic of Cancer*.

I continue typing the story she's indentured me to write.

I suppose I've thrown you, dear reader, into my life the same way this Faerie invaded it, so let me back up. Just until last week, so you can get the whole picture.

I was at a poker game in the back room of Flannigan's Bar. It's right around the corner from my house, and I like to go every Tuesday when they have poker games in the back room. And Thursdays when they have whiskey on special, and Monday—oh shit. I'm there just about every night. Don't judge me; you probably have some perverted habit like reading Jane Austin or maybe you collect clown figurines. Let's leave it and get on with the story. I was there at Flannigan's on a Tuesday night in the back room playing poker when this very pretty—actually really fucking beautiful—woman walks into the room. She's laughing it up with Donal, the bartender, who opened the door for her. She sits down and promptly starts slaying us. I mean, outright blood fest of cards. Finally there I am, shit for money, and she asks, if I don't have anything else to bet, what can I do instead? I say I'm a writer; I'll write something for her. And lo and behold, here I am, bet lost, writing a story for what ends up being a faerie. A real one, and I know she's tricked me. She must have cheated because I'm good at cards, real good.

Fast-forward to today, and you've got me stuck with a faerie living in my very small apartment—and her ignoring me like she normally does.

Faeries hate to be wrong. They like to always be right.

"What? That's not true." Juniper looks at me like I'm crazy. "Yes, it is true. You always contradict what I say." "Well," she says and sniffs, "I can't help it if you are stupid."

Faeries hate to be wrong. They like to be right always, and so Wendolyn did not say anything to anyone about the feeling the human girl gave her. She decided, under the pretext of getting more pollen, that she would go study the human once again.

"But haven't we got enough pollen?" asked her very nosy cousin, Missy Ronwen Moonbeam, flinging her long blue-silver hair.

"We need just a bit more," answered Wendolyn.

"I'll keep you company then." Ronwen could be very annoying.

"Not this time. I need to work fast, and you hold me back." With this and the snap of her fingers, Wendolyn was gone, not letting Ronwen have another word.

Wendolyn was a little nervous; heading toward humans went against everything she'd been taught. It was the lazy faeries, the arrogant ones, and also the drunk ones that got caught, and getting caught was one of the very worst things a faerie could do. Wendolyn was fast, and she was smart, and she would not get caught. She perched on the bottom of a redwood, the one closest to the tent. She heard voices inside the obtrusion and determined there were two females, and the new voice was the older one. Not old to a faerie, who could live for five hundred years.

Missy Wendolyn's body began to reverberate again, this time even more. She knew it was because of the other human; she also was made of the same stuff as the little girl. Quickly and quietly, she crept closer to the tent and perched on a blade of grass. She delicately balanced on a single blade with the grace of a ballerina. This was as close as she'd ever been to humans, and her heart pounded in her chest.

The woman's voice was wonderful, and it became clear to Wendolyn she was telling a story. She concentrated over the sound of her heart to hear what this warm voice had to say.

"The father of the faeries knew he had to protect his realm, but he also knew it would be hard," said the voice.

"What was the name of the father faerie?" asked a much younger voice.

"Hmmmm, how about uh, Master, um, Master Reginold Earthprotector?"

Wendolyn gasped, then immediately covered her mouth, fearing they'd hear her. Master Reginold Earthprotector was the name of the father faerie who had indeed saved the faerie realm in the Old World, one of the first great battles the faerie kingdom had ever seen.

Wendolyn listened with bated breath. The voice continued. "So anyway, Master Reginold Earthprotector was tired of getting bullied around by the ogres. Hey, my spine tickles; could you scratch if for me?"

Wendolyn's heart kept its frantic pace.

Replied the younger voice, "Do you mean like your spine is twitching like a, like a, a guitar string?"

"Yes, did we both get bit by something?" mused the disembodied voice from within the obtrusion.

"Mom, maybe it's faeries!" exclaimed the younger voice. The excitement bubbled in her throat.

Wendolyn couldn't listen anymore. They'd felt what she had, and the older human was talking about history no human should ever know. This was most alarming, and the faerie queen, Queen Arum the Brave and Gentle Heartsong, needed to be informed.

As the faerie crept away, the O'Malley females felt the tingling fade away, which baffled them even more.

Faeries are not the most organized.

H ow do you know?" asks Juniper.

"Because you've been here a week and still haven't folded your laundry," I reply.

B ut this does not mean they are not productive. Faeries keep themselves very busy, and their primary export is their coins. After crossing over to her realm—

"A h, the ethereal vortex?" I ask.

"Yes, now shut up and let me speak," Juniper replies.

W endolyn rushed through the vortex; she rushed past her cousin who was—

"I 'm not going to write that Wendolyn passed her cousin who was in an orgy." I say.

"Why the hell not?" she replies.

"Because it's inappropriate!" I say. I mean, this is a kid's story right? Or maybe not, but shit, I don't feel like writing about faerie sex.

"What a prude. One day in Faerie, and all your weird hang-ups would be gone. We do things you can't even imagine. Just thinking about it gives me the moisties. Besides, everyone knows Ronwen was one of the biggest sluts in town."

"We are moving on now," I say, desperate to get off this topic.

After crossing over to her realm, Wendolyn passed her friends and relations and went on to the kingdom.

The kingdom, oh the kingdom was a sight to see! It was as if the faeries lived among the human world but on another dimension. Trees growing out of other trees, with greens humans have never seen before. Their colors do not have names, at least not in human language. Flowers with pinks, oranges, and reds that would make a human actually feel like the colors, not just see them. Leaves with fragrances so strong one's skin would get wet. Plants that were light to the touch and sparkled like glass. Grass that moved and swayed like ocean waves. And the faeries! The faeries themselves, some working on coin or cloth, some playing or sleeping or eating, but all of them created a frenzy of excitement. It was a sight that only two humans had seen in the three hundred years they'd crossed over from the Old World. Each of them had met with an untimely death, as faeries are very protective of their world.

Faeries do not need much money, but kings and queens from other realms were partial to faerie coins, and it came in handy when bribing humans. Once brought into the human world, it looked like nothing more than normal gold, except that if one placed a piece of it seven feet under the ground and let it sit for seven days, it would double in amount. Usually a faerie could trick the human out of the gold promised, but the few times a human succeeded in keeping the gold, he led a happy and prosperous life.

"So, how did the two humans get into Faerie?" I ask over a meal of macaroni and cheese.

"In order to enter Faerie, one must be asked, or tricked—"

"As faeries are known to do." I cut her off, not hiding my annoyance.

"But on these two occasions that the humans weren't asked or tricked—"

"Like me?" I chime in loudly.

She's on a roll and continues, "Look, we protect our kingdom with spells. You can't get through the ethereal vortex, the portal if you will, unless you break the spells, but these two fools were so insufferably intoxicated and failed to get befuddled by the spells that hide the kingdom, as they'd befuddled themselves with whiskey."

Here she pauses and takes a sip of whiskey herself. For that matter, so do I.

"If these two hapless humans had not been so sauced out of their minds, the spells cast to protect the portal to Faerie would have made them feel very tired, lost, and lonely, eventually leading them to conclude that leaving this forest would be the best idea. Unfortunately, this didn't happen. They stumbled their way in but were quickly led out and were found the next day, cold and stiff with death, but with smiles on their faces. We can be fierce, but we are also kind."

"I have yet to see that," I say darkly.

"Go stick a hot poker where the sun don't shine, sister," replies Juniper.

My point exactly.

"Can I get on with it now? I have to go to work in an hour."

"Can you just *not* go? This is much more important."

"If I don't go to work, then I don't have money, and if I don't have money, then I can't buy raspberry vodka. If you'd give me a few of those damn faerie coins your type makes, then we'd be fine, but since you won't—and you've drunk all my vodka already—I have to go to work."

Juniper stares at me, and believe it or not, I am a little frightened, fierce little thing. She is like a lioness in a kitten's body.

"Get some fucking fruit on your way home."

I throw a pillow at her, stupid faerie.

My life was a nice strict routine: work, home, coffee shop, and Flannigan's. My stupid job is just so I have money to pay rent. My home is my sanctuary, and I go to the coffee shop to work on my novel, which is currently nothing at all. But it will be something as soon I get motivated again. Flannigan's is my relaxation and social time. I even meet up with a few people from work there from time to time. And then Juniper moved in, and not only is my house a disaster but she even goes with me to the coffee shop, which I hate because there is the Cutie-Pie, and next to her, I must look like a fucking mess. She walks me to work sometimes, and even likes to go to the grocery store. She's like a kid in a candy shop with even the littlest things. You should have seen her with the crosswalk button. What is strange is that she seems to know old and archaic technology but nothing made within the last seventy-five plus years. I guess fairies don't hang with humans much anymore. Not that I blame them, and honestly some of the things she points out about us I'd like to take to Congress. On the rare occasions that she won't come along, she is wrapped up in a book or is discovering music. I can't fault her for that; imagine living without rock 'n' roll. Holy shit, I'd go crazy.

So I walk to the corner store on my way home and get a bagful of fruit. I will say this, of course not in front of her, since she's been living with me, I've eaten better. I still love my mac and cheese and my pizza, but now I eat fruit and veggies like everyday. I suppose that's a bonus. I've also saved money on drinks since I'm not buying them at Flannigan's every night. Okay, so two good things have come out of this. Oh, and I've been writing. Never mind that it's not what I want to write; the point is, I'm getting words on the page, and that's better than I've done in the past six months. Still, I slow down the last block toward home because I just don't feel like having someone in my home, in my sanctuary.

Missy Wendolyn flew on through and did not stop even when nosy Missy Ronwen Moonbeam called out her name. On she went to the center of Faerie, to a castle that looked like fragile glass awash with translucent sunshine. It shimmered in the sun as if alive, or like a mirage. Yet to the touch, the walls would feel smooth and hard like marble, but warm. For a human, it would be as close as one could get to touching a sunbeam.

The castle was nestled among trees, almost as if it grew out of the trees, the bushes, and the ground that surrounded it. With each step, Wendolyn's feet made little dents in the golden light, and even though she'd been inside the castle hundreds of times, the sweet smell of cinnamon still surprised her.

She rushed past the guards and went up the steps despite their protests until she came to the grand doors, the doors that led to the throne room. Here, two guards stood outside the great doors, the thick, wooden doors that were carved over a span of years telling the story of Master Reginold Earthprotector. Having run quickly through the palace, Wendolyn stopped in front of the two formidable bodies that guarded the Throne Room. These were True Warriors. They came from warrior families, a bloodline that started thousands of years ago. There was no reckoning with these warriors. Their reputation was vicious, and they were known for the blood they could spill: faerie, elf, dwarf, ghoul, or even monster.

Wendolyn bowed respectfully to the warriors guarding the doors. "Is she in?" she asked, half-expecting to be turned away.

Without speaking, the two True Warriors opened the doors to the throne room. Imagine such large and heavy doors slowly opening, allowing for the room inside to be revealed. A large, long hall with pillars lining the sides and murals beyond the pillars, telling the history of the warriors, princes, and queens of time past, forever alive on these walls; this was where the queen held court.

The ceiling was rounded and transparent at night, and the stars happily shone in, but when Wendolyn entered, it was day and the ceiling was a continuation of the murals and delicate artwork that lined the walls. The throne itself was simple but elegant and up on a platform high enough so that even if the room were full, anyone could see the queen.

The steps leading to the throne also appeared to be made of golden light, like the ones leading up to the castle. And then, on the simple throne in this room so majestic, sat the queen, Queen Arum Heartsong. A vision to be sure, this faerie was particularly entrancing. Purple and silver hair, gray eyes, a strong jaw line, and tall, she was a good leader. Her dress shimmered, a different color revealed to everyone. It appeared delicate; the bodice looked as if spiders had spun it directly onto her body, intricate and detailed.

It took Missy Wendolyn a moment to gather herself as she stood in front of the queen. Despite having seen her many times before, Queen Arum had a way of taking one's breath away. Her regal presence left no room for uncertainty, and she would not tolerate wasted time. Unless, of course, she wanted to. Queen Arum was known to have been a great trickster in her earlier years, and on special occasions—namely parties and celebrations—she'd been known to throw her hair back and tell dirty jokes. But this was not one of those times, and Missy Wendolyn knew it. When the queen was in this room, when one asked to seek her advice, it was to be taken with the utmost respect that she'd allowed one into her schedule.

Queen Arum Heartsong did not move a muscle while listening to Wendolyn's tale. Faeries tend to lean toward exaggerated emotions.

"**W**hat? No we don't!" says Juniper as she reads over my shoulder. "We are just very *expressive*." she continues.

"No shit," I say.

Instead of a verbal rebuttal, Juniper makes a vase fly off the shelf and crash onto the ground. Sometimes I want to kill her.

B ut the rulers of such realms have to be composed and ready for complicated meetings with other creatures. Take the Treaty of 1410 for example. A clear head and cool exterior got the ogres to stop wreaking havoc on Faerie realm.

Wendolyn, on the other hand, could not contain herself. She told of her sighting the humans and of how they made her feel all the while doing a little hop-skip dance. When she noticed what she was doing, she'd force herself to stop, but then she'd get so worked up again and be hopping and skipping all over the place.

"It was the girl at first, you see. I've never felt that kind of tingle before, and I thought maybe they were half-breeds. I'd never felt it before, but then I was never that close to the little girl," started Wendolyn.

"But then when the mother, I think it was the mother, when she started talking about Sir Reginold Earthprotector, I mean, well, that was unusual, right?" She looked up at the queen to make sure this indeed was unusual.

The queen nodded and smiled at Wendolyn. "You did a fine job, Missy Wendolyn Brightwing."

Wendolyn blushed at the compliment and bowed profusely all the way out the door.

When Wendolyn was gone and the giant doors had closed, Queen Arum snapped her fingers. Her trusted friend and advisor instantly appeared in front of the throne. Master Spidertamer was an old faerie—a kind faerie but a very shrewd faerie—and he'd helped Queen Arum negotiate some very tough truces between the faerie kingdom and the elves. It'd been an act of unimaginable patience and diligent work. For this exceptional work, Queen Arum kept him by her side and named him chief advisor.

Master Spidertamer bowed to his lovely queen. He was a handsome faerie, even at three hundred and ninety years of age, his long black hair tied back with a ribbon. He wore a black, pinstriped coat on his long and spindly body. His boots were shiny as if brand new despite their decades of wear. Queen Arum acknowledged the bow with a nod of her head and waved him forward. She sat upright in her throne and waited until Master Spidertamer reached her side. Again he bowed, and when he stood up, he asked, "You beckoned?"

The queen stood and replied, "Not here, Master Spidertamer. The Room of Stratagems." With that, she took Master Spidertamer's arm, and they walked out of the throne room, down the hall, and into the room where wars were planned, lands invaded, and kingdoms defended.

The queen barely finished sitting down when she said eagerly, "I think we may have found Her."

Master Spidertamer replied, "Who?"

"The One," the queen replied after a second of silence.

Master Spidertamer sat back in his high-backed chair, a chair of beauty, like all things in faerie realm, and seriously studied his queen.

"Well, if you don't like it, you write the fucking thing!" I answer one of her endless questions/insults. I lift the glass to my lips, realize it's empty, and put it back on the table, a little harder than needed. "I mean, really, why am I doing this? You can write, right?"

The faerie squints at me as if she hasn't even heard me. "Maybe you aren't drunk enough."

"I'm serious, why do you want me to write this?"

Juniper does her little hop, skip, and jump over to the counter where the vodka sits and pours some more into my glass. While she mixes in some juice, I cradle my head in my hands. Why? How? How had I lost that round? I'm normally a good poker player, I swear. I'm the one who usually walks away with the whole pot. I call it my second job; it's what funds my as-of-not-yet-written book, the book that I will someday write when writer's block lets up.

Juniper gently puts the glass down in front of me; did you know faeries are graceful in everything they do?

"It's a gift, and while I am superior to you in every way—and I *am*—well, we faeries don't especially know how to write."

"At all?"

"We don't write things down. Everything is passed down through oral traditions. And, well, I know the person for whom this is for will find it tremendously wonderful."

I look down at the drink Juniper had set down for me. "This is not going to make me write better; it's just going to give me an awful hangover," I say, only because I know I won't get any more out of her on any other topic.

Juniper waves this comment away, like a fly.

"Faeries don't get hangovers, do they?" I ask.

"Don't worry. I'll give you something to ease the pain. Now let me tell you about the Stone."

I roll my eyes and sit back with a pad of paper and a pen to take notes. The notes on Faerie and the O'Malley family have already filled a whole Mead notebook, and I'm on the second.

"See, everything has a gender. Living things like streams, trees, rocks, and mountains are obvious, and they speak to us. Inanimate objects have only a semblance of what they were, so if a table came from a male tree, I'd call it he."

Ah, that explains why she always calls my table him.

"What's my door?" I ask.

"It had a sex change. It's now a her."

"Really?" My surprise shows easily.

Juniper rolls her eyes. "No, you git. How can a tree have a sex change? It's a female."

"What about the lamp?"

She sighs. "Can we please get to the story? I'll indulge your curiosities later."

Grumpily, I hunker down in my male-or-female chair and begin to write while Juniper narrates.

"The She that the queen spoke of was a pendant, an old crystal that had magic woven into it for many years. It was one of the five most powerful Magics a faerie could possess, and it had been lost for hundreds of years, on its crossing from the motherland."

"On the crossing from the motherland?" I ask, raising my eyebrows.

Juniper, not getting my sarcasm, stares at me.

"You think I write like a Victorian novel? Jesus, looks like the broom is up your ass now."

She stands up angrily. "Oh, shut your gob. What you do know anyway?"

You'd think I was used to her yelling at me, but this time, it catches me off guard, and I do shut up. I'm not pathetic, just poor and lonely and as of yet unpublished. That's not pathetic, right?

Missy Pine Hollowtree was not a bad faerie. She was actually a very good faerie. She was kind and sweet and always willing to help a fellow being. Unfortunately, it was this goodness of heart that got her into trouble—a trouble she didn't even know she was in. Missy

Pine saw the queen and her advisor enter the Stratagem Room, and hastily with her Sound Bubble, followed behind them. With a quick motion, she rolled the bubble inside the room and waited behind a wall.

Everything said between the queen and Master Spidertamer would be recorded in the Sound Bubble that she would then give to the Dark King. Had she realized this could bring down the kingdom she loved so much and hurt the queen she served so faithfully, her heart would have broken a million times over. The spell the Dark King had woven on her pretty little head made sure she wouldn't remember any of her actions. Happily she skipped along, following orders from the faerie that could destroy her world.

Ever since the Dark King came to be, Faerie had been ripped in two. King Heartstrong, and later his daughter Queen Arum, ruled the Light faeries. The Dark King ruled the Dark faeries. His kingdom was far beyond the boundaries of Queen Arum's realm, past the Forest of Blood Trees, where no self-respecting being would venture.

Imagine one's life filthy with violence. A childhood spent under a bed listening to the cries of mother. A lonely adolescence after mother was dealt the final blow and left with the hatred of human kind imbued in father. This is not living. It is a slow death of the heart. One must understand the Man (who became the Dark King) had many reasons to have an empty soul. The triumphs of those who overcome similar adversity are miracles in a graveyard of spent lives. The human heart can only withstand so much hate before reaching a critical point wherein it ceases to beat to the sound of love. No. It thrives on pain, rage, and fear. Every person turned to such thoughts is a tragedy. The heart beats out rhythms of hate, propelling men turned into the walking dead, sucking the soul out of life.

Shall the Man have a name? Indeed, he did as a human. Although it should not come as a surprise to learn he had long since forgotten it. Christopher. His name had been Christopher. A strong name his mother had bestowed on him in hopes he could transcend the pit of despair she had brought him into. Named after the patron saint of travelers. Travel he did. Into the world of the surreal, and most likely, no one of holy nature was watching. If they had been watching, their hearts would be heavy with the sadness that his soul was empty.

"Wait, so the bad guy was a human? I'm confused."

"At first. Then he became a faerie king. I'm just trying to introduce to you the Dark King. But let's get back to the queen and Master Spidertamer," said Juniper.

Like that cleared anything up.

The queen waited impatiently for Master Spidertamer to speak. His thoughts had taken him far into his own mind, but finally he shook himself into the present and said, very seriously, "Is it really possible? It has been lost for so many years; how can we be sure? And where do you think it may be?"

"Speak with Missy Wendolyn. She sensed magic around humans! They could be the Lost Faerie Children." The queen paused for a moment. "There haven't been any affairs between humans and faeries, at least none that I know of. It could be that these humans are the product of some wayward love affair. But what if they are the two that Mistresses Lily Brightwater and Osmunda and Master Willow Wildbrook hid away?"

Master Spidertamer had a hard time masking his doubt. The children and their guardians had been lost to the faeries in an attempt to keep the Crystal safe. He didn't even know if they were alive, and now to think they were, and living as humans … it seemed far-fetched. It did not take the queen's refined insight to see it behind his eyes.

"Your doubt is well founded. You will suggest we send a spy to the house to see more of this human family."

"Yes, I would advise it," he said.

The queen nodded, just once, very regally and decisively. "I will go."

Master Spidertamer sputtered in surprise.

"No, my queen, you may not! The risk is too great!"

The queen stood, and her skirts swished around her.

"I will go, and that is final. You know we cannot afford to tell anyone about this. Should the Dark King find out, our kingdom could be destroyed forever."

"Then bring with you two guards—"

"I said no one must hear of this. Between you and me only."

"Do you not trust your loyal servants?" Master Spidertamer was desperate to keep his queen safe. Looking at her mentor, she stopped the quick and scathing rebuttal shaped on her tongue. Instead, she smiled.

"Old friend, it is not that I do not trust anyone; it is that I do not trust the Dark King. It has been the length of human lives since we've heard from him, and I fear the calm before the storm. Is it strange that we've suddenly heard this tale exactly one hundred years after the disappearance?"

"We are not sure it is the Crystal. Perhaps these humans are the children of wayward lovers; we just don't know."

"Precisely why I must go and see. Imagine the Dark King capturing whomever we send out there—"

Master Spidertamer could not help but interrupt. "Exactly why we should send someone other than you!"

"That is enough! Should the Dark King gain the Crystal, we are dead or worse, under his rule. This is too great a risk to allow anyone else to do. I—only I—alone will go. Your presence is no longer required."

She snapped her fingers, and instantly Master Spidertamer found himself in his study, alone with worries, swimming through his thoughts and the knowledge that his queen would do as she wished, just as she had done ever since she was a child.

I'm finally allowed a moment alone. Juniper has invaded my life, and most days I feel like I can't even breathe. I left her in my living room, with records and CDs splayed around her because she's attempting to make her first mix tape. She didn't tell me whom it's for. In fact, she shooed me out of my own apartment like I'm the one who stormed in and took over her place.

Images from the story Juniper is dictating to me fill my head, and I can't shake these characters from my mind. Are these nonhuman creatures real? Juniper is real, and believe me, I would not have believed faeries were real until I met her.

I get to the coffee shop, grateful for the warmth that greets me. It's a sweet little mom and pop place, not sterile and streamlined. It's not country kitsch with flowery curtains. No, nothing like that. The walls are painted muted colors with rotating art tastefully hung on them. Right now, there is a series of skateboards, old broken skateboards with landscapes painted on them. If I had the money, I would totally buy one; they are that good. The tables don't match, the chairs don't match, but they are all nicely kept, so it doesn't look like someone's dumpster run. Plants and cleverly placed bookcases create little nooks in which to lose oneself in a book or conversation.

There are a few tables that line the back wall, where all the cool web designers and graphic artists sit. Writers too. I've set up my laptop on one of those tables many a time.

And there he is—Cutie Pie—Buddy Holly glasses, sweater, and laptop. There is a cowlick that makes his dark brown hair stick up in a disheveled-but-still-cute kind of way. Damn. I sneak a peek at my outfit and realize my sweater is buttoned wrong and remember too late that the hat I shoved onto my head has a hole on the side.

I sigh inwardly and move to the counter, wishing so much he won't see me.

Jen, all kinds of cute with a nose ring and big anime eyes, bops to the beat of the music, and she smiles when she sees me as she hands a customer a hot beverage.

I wait my turn, willing myself to not look over my shoulder. I know the moment I break down and look in his direction, he'll look up. And I'll probably—right at that moment—have to sneeze and blow snot all over my hands. Or someone will walk by and spill his double mocha all over me. Or some hot girl will walk in, stand next to me, and dwarf any chance I have at looking cute. Yeah, better not turn around.

"Charlotte, how's it going?" It's my turn, and Jen has to get my attention back to reality.

Jen always has a smile on her face; I don't get how she does it. Once I watched as someone reamed her for a lukewarm latte, and she just smiled, apologized, and made a new one. For the record, I was screaming my head off—in my mind—at the rude patron, and by the time it was my turn to order, I was red in the face. Jen just laughed when I asked her about it. "People just want to be important, and if that means I have to make a lousy latte again ... well ... I hope it helped them feel better."

Are you shitting me? People like Jen really exist? I think I'd lose my job the first day because I could never be so damn Zen.

"How are you anyway?" she asks.

"I'm f-f-fine."

"Where's your friend?"

I roll my eyes.

"Is she your roommate?" Jen prods.

"Y-y-ou could s-say that."

Jen takes my money, and as she makes my drink, I do it without even realizing I'm doing it. I turn around.

And he looks up.

But I don't sneeze snot all over my hands, no one spills a drink on me, and no hottie walks through the door.

We just stare at each other, and I'm so self-conscious, but I also don't want to look away, so I keep staring until I realize Jen is talking to me.

"Here ya go, double short, no foam."

I turn back around, dazed. Jeez, I feel like a schoolgirl crushing for the first time.   I must have blushed because Jen gives me a Look.

"You think he's cute?"

I shrug and shake my head, hoping that's enough of an answer. Jen winks at me and thanks me for the tip I leave in the jar.

I avoid looking in his direction as I walk back out into the cold.

I'm sort of sweating in my winter clothes, and the cold air feels good after the stuffy coffee shop.

It also helps calm me from the giddy tummy I have.

The three blocks home are full of Cutie Pie's eyes framed in those glasses. Damn me. Damn him! I reach my building and look up. The window to my apartment is open, and I hear strains of music floating on the wind. I listen, trying to pick out what the song is.

Because the night belongs to lovers
Because the night belongs to us ...

She has discovered Patti Smith and I smile. Coming home to my rock hero blasting from the stereo gives me strength to go up the stairs and confront the abnormality in my life. Until I open the door.

"You humans are horrible to each other. You'd think you'd be nicer when you've only got less than a hundred years to live."

This coming from the faerie who froze her cousin for a whole week—for stealing her favorite leather jacket. Hypocrisy must not be a word in Faerie vocabulary.

I try to ignore her as I take off my coat, scarf, and hat with the hole in it and hang them up on the coatrack. I head to the kitchen, where it looks like she's been making herself a sandwich of carrots, peanut butter, and nutmeg.

"I just came home? A hello before your next tirade might be nice," I tell her, plopping down in a chair and putting my latte on the table.

"I was reading this book." She holds up Agatha Christie. Juniper is learning human behaviors from Agatha Christie? I can't help but laugh.

"First of all, this was the 1920s. Secondly, it's fiction, and thirdly, you hold a double standard for us humans and you faeries. You get into fights over the pettiest things; you kill humans that stray into your world, but then we are the violent ones?" I say.

"We don't kill unless we have to, and I can assure you those two humans died way happier then anyone in these books." She motions to the Agatha Christie book.

"Besides, we don't kill each other, almost never. You'd think because your life is so short, you humans would learn how to get along." She takes a bite of her sandwich … it actually smells really good.

"Stop making excuses. The fights you and your cousin have gotten into are downright vicious," I say.

Juniper sniffs and continues to eat as if nothing I say means a thing. "You should know, before you judge us, that we are bloody awesome at parties. It's been recorded that the longest faerie party lasted no less than thirty-two days, with thirty-three barrels of whiskey, twenty gallons of lemongrass soup, three whole pigs, a goat, and twenty-three pounds of fruit and vegetables. And we don't have such rigid restrictions on copulation. Sex for everyone, I say. So there, stupid human."

So there? Is she fourteen?

"Nobody says copulation anymore." That's all I can come up with.

But she ignores me and goes to the laptop on the kitchen table where I guess she'd been reading what I had so far. She plops the mystery novel beside the computer and begins to eat and read, while I sip my latte and dream of Cutie Pie.

Juniper nods after she reads a while and says, "That's very accurate. I guess you do listen."

Trying to show her that I don't care if she likes it, I grumpily reply, "Yeah, well, I told you I'm good."

"Between magic and precise craftsmanship, faeries are extraordinary seamstresses and tailors. In addition to our coins, a major export is our cloth. The elves might be known for their sewing, but in the end, they need our cloth to make their clothes. Trying to describe it in your words sullies the very nature of our craftsmanship," she explains to me.

I look down at my secondhand outfit, which I'd been proud of this morning.

Juniper must have seen my embarrassment because she takes off the scarf she's wearing and gently winds it around my neck.

"I'm not a charity case," I say, trying to play off my discomfort.

The truth is, the scarf feels heavenly. The texture is not like cloth but more like a feeling; it feels like joy. On Juniper, it had a distinct greenish hue, but on me, it's turned blue, purple, and gold all at once. I look at her, surprised.

She smiles. "Faerie cloth, once you start, you can't stop."

I smile back, and as I stroke it, my fingers tingle; suddenly, I don't hate the faerie quite so much.

The Dark King sat in his Dark Throne Room. He was brooding as usual. Not even the torture he enacted upon one of his subjects could bring him out of his foul mood. All his servants were careful not to approach him or even look at him. It was baffling then to see a Light faerie skipping down the halls happily.

Missy Pine Hollowtree was pleased that she had something to share with the Dark King. The Sound Bubble was safely tucked in her pocket with her hand resting over it, keeping it safe.

The presence of a Light faerie in Dark realm was shocking; perhaps it was the first time in history. The guards at the doors of the throne room stopped the Light faerie, unsure why she was there or how to treat her.

"I request an interview with Oh Lord of the Dark, with He Who Became King."

"Have you an appointment?"

"I was told by the king that I have only to say my name, and the guards shall let me pass."

"Your name, little Light faerie?"

"Missy Pine Hollowtree."

"Pass and may you gain what you seek."

One thing Pine loved about being a faerie was all the old traditions. She would have to review that poem—or was it a song? No, it was a poem about the birth of tradition. It just made everything so official and handsome—

"Yes?" The Dark King interrupted her thoughts. The stupid Light faerie looked so eager, so ready to be helpful. If only she knew how she was helping him destroy her precious realm!

"O, Dark King, I have news that thou will most certainly be seeking."

"Just tell me!" Her flowery language had a way of getting on his nerves. He preferred much more to get to the point, and he hated all the traditional brouhaha these faeries insisted upon. If he—no, *when*—he became king of all Faerie, things would change. Oh, yes, things would change.

"So you guys don't have any books?" I ask. We are walking briskly, hot chocolates in hand.

I am wearing the scarf Juniper gave me. Point of fact, I haven't taken it off since she wound it around my neck.

"While the scholarly faeries like to collect books from other creatures—humans included—we do not write books. We do not have history books, or any books for that matter, mainly due to the fact that—"

"You don't know when to end a story?" I razz her.

Dark looks from my companion, who, by the way, is getting stared at by every man who walks by. And woman. And child. And dog. You get the point.

It sounds silly—I know—that after the three short weeks since I met her, I know so much about faerie behavior, but until you've sat with one and waited five hours for her to finish an anecdote, you will understand what I mean. She doesn't know when to finish a story. In between her telling me about Maggie, Queen Arum, and Wendolyn, I've had to sit through hours of her own personal history, like the time she had a three-way in a tree—don't ask—or about the time she and her cousin got lost because they were too drunk to remember which way was north.

"All our lessons in history are passed down in the old oral tradition of song and verse," continues Juniper. "We faeries enjoy singing and reciting very much, and also, what would happen if others got a hold of our stories, histories, and secrets? Or maybe the younger generations would forget history because they were not taught to recite it all? I see you humans; you've all made the same mistakes over and over and over, and when you all realize it, it doesn't matter because it's the next generation who does it all over again! Proof that humans are stupid and stubborn."

"You know, we aren't that stupid; you had to find a human to write your dumb little novel—"

She cuts me off. "This isn't a novel, it's nonfiction."

"Well, whatever it is, I'm the one doing it—not you."

She doesn't answer but takes a sip of her hot chocolate.

We walk in silence a little more; we are getting closer to the god-awful building I call work. My stomach drops. I hate this building. I hate sitting on the computer, taking in orders for Christmas shit, Halloween shit, Easter shit, Thanksgiving shit, and all other fucking crap people want to spend their money on.

"I guess you guys end up memorizing a lot?" I prolong the conversation so I don't have to think about work.

"All faeries learn the required three thousand songs and poems that make our history."

"Three thousand?" And I thought it was hard learning *Jabberwocky* in eighth grade.

"Epic poems of grisly battles, sweet songs of peaceful times, quick limericks of sexual prowess, long songs of heroes, kings, and queens … you know, I used to read. When I lived—when I was little, I read many human books."

I look at her, and she is not with me on the sidewalk. She is deep in a memory, and she looks vulnerable for a moment. Turning toward the door, I sigh. I have to go in. I have to sit for six hours. I have to take orders for garbage made in China, and then I have to come home to this strange being.

"Try to puke and get excused from work," is how Juniper leaves me, skipping down the street.

I laugh because, if nothing, else my steady, stable world has wobbled, and just maybe, I'm having fun after all.

Master Spidertamer sat in his study. He sat entirely still. When one's life span is five hundred years, one learns that time is relative, and that it bodes well to do some serious thinking, which is what he was doing with his eyes unfocused, staring at the paintings on the wall.

War is a frightening thing, and there was nothing romantic about it. Their kingdom had lived in relatively peaceful times, and Master Spidertamer was anxious to keep it that way. Only having fought in skirmishes between realms, he knew he was not experienced in the ferocity that was needed for battle. Also, he didn't want the reign of his fair queen to be marred by such a tragedy.

Master Spidertamer sat in his study and thought about a poem. It was one in particular that told of the man who became the Dark King.

In a forest deep one day of ill fate
Met a faerie and a man full of hate.
His heart was shriveled and void of joy
Because of the violence he'd seen as a boy.
The wind howled a warning, the trees rustled with fear,
But they were not able to stop what was near.
In his human life, he learned to be quick,
To be slippery and sly and to do dirty tricks.
It was his training as a crook that he was able to hook
The unsuspecting faerie and three wishes he took.
The trees watched with horror as the man captured the faerie,
And tortured the creature with tactics too scary.
The wind kept on blowing in attempt to save,
But the faerie to the human had become a slave.
Three wishes he would have to bestow
On this man whose soul had ceased to glow.
The first to be king he demanded
To rule others he forcefully commanded.

Upon thinking it further it occurred to this king

That the power of magic was a much better thing.

The third of his wishes, for the second had been riches,

Was to become something even better than witches.

A faerie like his captive is what he wanted to be

And the faerie had no choice but to grant wish number three.

Despite pain and suffering, that faerie was smart,

And he took cursing to a whole new art.

Hidden in the king's wish to alter

Was a mechanism for his magic to falter.

The Dark King would not be as strong

As long the Crystal to him did not belong.

All the hate the Dark One possessed

In equal amounts, goodness would rest

In the Stone turned to Crystal, the magic was woven

The perfect female rock had been chosen

To hide deep inside a pureness of love

The Dark King should never hear it spoken of.

Master Spidertamer reached a good stopping point in the poem. He got up to make some tea. He needed to stretch his legs and move his arms. As he was doing this, he received a summons from Queen Arum. She was ready to make her departure and needed to give him last-minute instructions. There was no spring in his step as he answered the queen's call. He knew what could happen if it was the Crystal that had surfaced. And what could happen if the Dark King found out. No good could come of that.

It was late, and the kingdom was quiet with sleep. Master Spidertamer looked out from the doors to the palace at the rolling hills beyond the last of the faerie houses. What he had worked so hard for could quickly come to ruin, and he took a moment to drink in a little bit of hope. He wished very much that the Crystal had not been found, but then contradicting himself, wished what the queen said was truth. If they, the Light Faeries, were the ones that found the Crystal, then the Dark King would forever be powerless.

Master Spidertamer had served Queen Arum since she was a young queen and her father before that. He was well versed in running the kingdom. He had a decent sense of what was right and good for the faeries as a whole. That was partly due to the queen's father, King Heartsong. He'd ruled with a steady but heavy hand. The queen had been a difficult child, an impulsive and overly mischievous one. Many worried she would not rise to the challenge when it came time for her to step into her father's place, but Master Spidertamer had always known that, despite her impish behavior, she would someday make a very good ruler. He was not wrong. Her love for her people showed in her taking on this task. It is true she could send someone else, but it was just like her to want to do it herself.

Master Spidertamer smiled to himself as he descended the steps of the palace, to his waiting queen, looking regal as always.

"You'd think passing history through poems and such would lend to better writing. Dr. Seuss could have done better," I say.

"Dr. Seuss only had your dumb English to work with. The poem about the Dark King sounds stupid in your language, but in ours, it is awe inspiring, truly masterful, and scary. Much better in our tongue, as is Dr. Seuss for that matter," says Juniper.

I don't know what surprises me more, that Juniper knows whom Dr. Seuss is or that they've translated him into their language.

"So tell me about this Crystal," I say, not wanting to get into the world of Faerie language.

"Okay. So this faerie that got tricked by the Dark King? He had the Insight," Juniper started.

"The what about what?" The fact that she tells me these things like I know what she's talking about makes me feel stupid. I don't like that.

"The Insight. It's where one can see the ... well, like the truth in a being's heart. Whether it is a beast or human or another supernatural. Anyway he, the faerie that got caught—"

"Do we know how he got caught?" I interrupt.

"No, actually no one really knows. The only reason we even know this chap existed is because the Dark King bragged about how he became a faerie king," says Juniper. "May I continue?"

"Go for it," I reply.

"After seeing the man's burned, shriveled heart inside his tight chest, the faerie took a stone and put the same amount of Goodness into this stone as the man had Badness in his heart. The stone now in possession of faerie power became a crystal, and not like any other in the world. The secret spell stipulated that the man-turned-faerie would not have full power until he destroyed the crystal. That is not to say he couldn't do magic—indeed, he could—but his magic was weak. Spells cast would not bind well or for very long, and he'd tire more quickly than others."

"So he's a faerie, can do magic, and is a badass, but he's slightly handicapped?" I ask.

"Yes, will you stop your infernal interrupting?" she asks while giving me a dirty look. I roll my eyes as she begins to speak again.

"This item now in possession of a huge amount of Goodness had many names: the Stone, the Crystal, the Pendant, and the She. The stone it was made from had been female."

"Then everything was okeydokey, right? I mean, if he can't live up to his full potential, then who cares?"

I suddenly get cold as if storm clouds had engulfed me because that is how cold her withering look is to me.

"Listen, dummy, clearly there is more to this story or else I wouldn't be here, slumming it with you, so if you don't mind, shut your gob so I can get on with my story."

I don't say anything. Better to let the storm pass even if I'm tempted to see how far I can push it.

"The Dark King didn't know about the Stone and had he never found out, things would be okay, I suppose. I mean, he still reined terror, maiming and torturing people he decided deserved it. But it wasn't nearly the mayhem he could have brought onto the entire world—not just Faerie—if he came into possession of the She. Somehow he found out about it, and that's where the trouble really began."

M aggie lay with her arms wrapped around her mother. *She looks so peaceful*, thought Maggie, *and beautiful.* She didn't want to stir her mother, whose striking eyes were concentrated on the ceiling of the tent. Maggie wondered what her mother was thinking and squeezed her tight to let her know she'd woken up.

Matilda looked over to her daughter and smiled.

"What were you thinking?" Maggie asked.

"Aunt Lily gave me a necklace a long time ago. I used to wear it all the time, and then one day, she told me to stop wearing it. I just remembered this."

"Why would she tell you to stop wearing it? Because it would break?" asked Maggie.

Matilda shrugged. "Maybe. We wrapped it in a scarf and then put it in an old hatbox. Honestly, I completely forgot about it till just now."

"Why?" asked Maggie.

"Why what?" asked Matilda.

"Why did you think of it?" asked Maggie.

"I had a dream about it. I also dreamt of a woman. She was like me, but it was not me, and she was sad."

Maggie squeezed her mother again. "I don't want you to be sad."

Again Matilda smiled at the sweet girl next to her. "I'm not sad, my little love. I'm very happy."

Both of them stirred when they heard footsteps outside the tent. For a moment, Maggie got lost in excitement; perhaps it was a faerie! But the realization that faeries would not clomp about—that most likely they would glide or fly or do anything more graceful than clomp—set her back into a funk, and a scowl met her father upon entering the tent.

"No faeries?" he asked his grumpy daughter.

"No."

"Well, how about some hot chocolate?" he said.

Maggie sat up; the prospect of her father's delicious morning beverage was almost enough to put a smile on her face.

Matilda also sat up, and the smell of fresh coffee teased her senses. Oh, how she loved the morning!

As they ate their breakfast, an old thought came to Matilda. "Robert, have you ever ... has anything jogged your memory about your parents?"

Robert smiled at his wife. It'd been a long time since they'd talked about this. As children, they'd always hashed and rehashed the few details they knew, the details they cherished as their only link to their parents.

"No, nothing. Are we ten again?" he answered.

"I still think it's strange that we remember so little." Matilda looked wistful as she played with Maggie's unruly hair. Maggie stayed quiet; she liked it when her parents spoke of the past.

"I had a dream last night ... remember that necklace I always used to wear?" said Matilda.

"With the silver chain and that odd crystal?" asked Robert.

"That's it. You remember it?"

"Vaguely."

"I had a dream about it last night. It was important." Matilda smiled; Maggie could tell she felt silly talking about her dreams. Her mother had once told Maggie dreams sometimes showed what was in your heart and were meant for you and you alone.

"Sounds like you've been telling magpie stories." Robert laughed at his wife's imagination.

Matilda laughed it off as well, but Maggie did not want to let it go. "What about the necklace? What did it look like? Was it Aunt Lily's? An old heirloom?" asked Maggie.

"Aunt Lily used to say, 'Forget the past. Memories of the past will become clear when it is time.' I never really understood what she meant by that," said Matilda.

"Don't old people like to talk about the good old days? Like Suzy's grandma, whenever she visits, me and Suzy have to sit *forever* listening to what it was like when *she* was a girl," Maggie said.

"There was a fire that leveled the town when she was a girl; there's no record of her birth. It was a strange detail to surface when I had to file for her death certificate, so I never knew how old she was. That seems so strange to me."

Matilda poured herself another cup of coffee and settled into her chair; Maggie sat in hers straight up, excited to get more history.

"Auntie Brightwater did not like to talk about the past. Every once in a long while, when Robert and his family would come over for dinner, she'd grow sentimental and speak of Ireland. Remember that, Robert?" Matilda turned toward her husband.

"They loved her stories. They would rehash them when we got home, remembering every word Aunt Lily said," said Robert with a smile.

"You haven't told me any of these stories!" Maggie said, surprised there were things she didn't know.

"I can't really remember the details," admitted Matilda. "I wish I could."

Maggie sighed, and for the millionth time in her young life, she wished Aunt Lily were still alive. There was so much she wanted to know.

The Who is breaking my concentration.
　　"Juniper! Damn it! Juniper!"

With eyes as bright as Christmas lights, Juniper dances about the living room.

"Do you hear this?" she says.

"Yes! Turn it down."

But she ignores me. Surprise, surprise. "It's the best thing in the whole world! I can't—I just can't turn it down."

I get up and stretch. Basically my options seem to be these: either the faerie hangs out in the living room with me and reads over my shoulder, she listens to my record collection with the volume blasting, or she stomps off angrily to my room and locks herself in there for hours.

"I can't concentrate with 'My Generation' stuttering in the background," I say.

Juniper dances around me like the drunken faerie she is and laughs.

Shaking my head, I make my way into the kitchen. It is a mess naturally; I don't have any time to clean while writing this story for the damn faerie.

Pushing dirty dishes aside, I find a bowl in the sink and begin to wash it. I'll have a bowl of cereal and then get back to work.

I sit at the table, staring off into space and listening to the music.

Juniper storms in with fire in her eyes and a CD in her hand. "Why do you have a compact disc of pixies?" she demands.

"It's a band." I try the you-are-stupid voice on her, but she's hopping around like she's stepping on burning coals.

"Why the fuck would you have a compact disc of pixies? Are they singing? They are horrible musicians. I can't believe you'd like their music after seeing your extremely cool record collection I'm sorely dis—"

"It's a *human* band," I yell over her tirade.

That stops her.

"Oh."

She examines it.

"Well, it's a stupid name, so, you know, they are probably lame."

I look at her amused. "I actually think you'd like them."

She tosses the CD on the table.

"No way I'd like them." With that, she turns around and returns to the living room.

I finish my cereal slowly, losing myself in thoughts unrelated to faeries, the story, or anything that surrounds me right now.

Thoughts take me to the coffee shop around the corner, the one that Cutie Pie also frequents. I think about the last guy I dated, and I shudder. Just because a guy can play the guitar does not mean he can string together an intelligent thought. Since moving here to the Big City, I've been on my own. I have friends, so don't pity me, and I talk to my brother and sister once a week. I'm not a hermit. I've only been here a few months, and with my stutter ... it just takes me longer.

I've thought about talking to Cutie Pie, but since I stutter horribly talking to anyone who doesn't have magic powers, I quietly walk by him four mornings a week. I'd just rather not, you know, have to talk to strangers.

There's a lull in the loud music, so I peek my head around the curtain that separates the living room from the kitchen. Juniper is intently looking at two records, trying to decide which one is next.

Grabbing the CD off the table, I glide in, quickly so she won't see, and put the disc in. I press play and Frank Black's voice blasts us.

Juniper looks up, startled by the music, but I can tell she likes it. Of course she does, this faerie has good taste in music. Her head bops along, and she forgets about the two record covers in her lap: Meat Puppets and Leonard Cohen (I told you good taste) and lets the music fill her up.

"Who is this?"

"The Pixies," I say with a smile. I know it will piss her off, but I also know she loves it. Ha! Got her this time.

She jumps up and is about to yell, but then "Wave of Mutilation" comes on, and I know she's defeated. The smile on her face is too much.

"Yeah, okay, human. You're right. It's bloody brilliant."

Maggie convinced her mother they had to look for the necklace that had appeared in her mother's dream, which was deep in the attic. Maggie loved to explore the corners, dark and mysterious. Rarely was she allowed up in the attic, and usually, it was for specific purposes like the Christmas decorations or the Halloween skeletons, all things that were right at the entrance, and did not require any savaging. Hunting down the aisles of piled boxes was a treasure in and of itself, even if there was nothing to bring down in the end. The smells of musk and lavender were left over from Aunt Lily, at least that's what her mother told tell her. The two of them gaily pulled out old clothes, shoes, hats, and a jumble of Aunt Lily's things that Matilda hadn't been able to part with.

Finally, Matilda came to the box the necklace was in and immediately felt a tingle. So did Maggie; a tingle that ran from her heart all the way down to her toes and up again to her head. It felt like electricity. The strangeness was not lost on either O'Malley, and Maggie shuffled closer to her mother. There was something more here, and though Maggie didn't know what it was, she knew it was different from anything she'd ever heard about. Saying good-bye to the other delights in the attic, Maggie followed her mother to her parents' bedroom, where an antique full-length mirror stood sentinel in the corner.

As Matilda pulled a necklace made of the finest silver from the scarf it'd resided in all these years, the crystal that hung on the delicate chain winked in the light. At first, it looked blue to Maggie, and then green, and then a sort of gold color. It seemed the closer she looked at it, the more it would change. A sort of longing fell over Maggie, a pull to something, but she couldn't put a name to it. It was a strong feeling, and it made her a bit sad.

She looked to her mother and was struck by how sad she looked. Impulsively, she gave her mother a hug, sandwiching the necklace between them. When the necklace touched her skin, instantly her heart calmed down. She pulled apart from her mom.

"Try it on. Try it on!" she insisted, and when her mother clasped it on, her natural radiance seemed a bit brighter. Her skin emitted light somehow, her hair shone. Maggie oohed and ahhed at her mother, the rare compliments Matilda treasured so much.

After a little looking in the mirror, Matilda pulled her daughter in front of it and put the necklace on her. The same thing happened. All that was Maggie seemed just a bit more, and Maggie was stunned into silence. She shone like her mother had and felt peaceful.

Robert came into the room to see what all the commotion was about because even he'd felt the tug Matilda had. The sight of his girls awed him as always, and he sat down on the bed to watch them. The three of them studied the necklace; they couldn't decide if the intricate chain was made of silver. Each link looked handmade, and they wove around each other with such detail it did not seem fathomable that anyone could actually make it. And no one could agree on the color of the crystal—or even if it was crystal.

Maggie sat between her parents and became a little frightened. She could sense her parents were uneasy. She knew if she said anything, they would reassure her with platitudes despite their own unease.

The O'Malleys were not the only ones who felt the surge. As Queen Arum approached the house, her body tensed involuntarily. The Crystal was near, and it was touching faerie skin. *What faerie?* she wondered as she neared the human dwelling.

A horrible thought rushed through her: *Is the Dark King here? No,* she thought, after examining the tingles. It was not black magic she felt; it was neutral, as if those radiating it were unaware of the magic they produced.

This required a serious think before she went and spoke with these humans. If they were indeed the lost faerie children, they may have forgotten who they really are—or they may be pixies or some other sort of supernatural being. Elves! Oh, if they were witches, they'd demand a hefty price for the Crystal.

Queen Arum would not allow herself to get caught and grant wishes. She was not about to put her realm in jeopardy. One thing she knew for sure: the Stone was inside, and she had to get it, but any rushed decisions could lead to regrets. She would get a good look at these creatures, be they human or faerie or both, and then she would go back to her kingdom and speak with Master Spidertamer. They could hash out a plan together.

Today! Today is the day of glory, thought the sinister Dark King. He had been waiting for so long. Sometimes he was almost sure it would never happen.

He thought of the faerie that had cursed him with his spell. *That little twerp!*

The Dark King had been tricked, and he didn't like being tricked. In fact, he didn't like anything that didn't directly benefit him, and being cursed did not benefit him. He thought back to the time he had almost acquired the She, the time he left so many dead in his wake.

For weeks, months, and years, he had searched, tortured, maimed, and killed to find the Stone, and it wasn't until it was almost too late that he found out that the Pendant was leaving the country.

All those years ago, They Who Guard the Stone left the old country by ship to take the Crystal to the New Country, hoping they could find a safe place for it. They changed into human shape for the trip. There were six of them: two sets of males and females and each with one child. He knew they would try to ship the She off to the New World, thinking it would be safer with an ocean between him and the Stone. He knew this after ripping the wings off of a high-level official within the palace. Of course, that poor faerie died, but only after days of agonizing pain. No faerie can rebuild its wings, and the slow death is nothing any decent faerie would wish on anyone, except maybe the Dark King himself.

After spending weeks scouring the docks, buying drinks, and treating captains to lavish meals, he finally found out that two families were to board in a day's time. He wanted their names off the passenger manifest.

When he found out about the voyage, he immediately took passage as a crewmember.

The Dark King had also changed to human form, but his advantage was that he'd been human and understood humans far better than faeries. While his magic was weak, his art of deception was keen, and he fit right in.

The passengers and crew regarded the faeries as strange. Had they been asked why, their answers would have been vague: wisps of ideas would float in their minds, but not tangible enough for a full thought. They were odd, these two couples and their children. Wasn't it strange the way they dressed in outdated clothes? Yet they were the handsomest people the rest of the passengers had ever met.

The Dark King fit right in as a deckhand, and he worked just as hard. He knew faeries could sense magic; not once throughout the whole voyage did he use a single spell. While he knew who they were, they hadn't any idea who he was, an advantage he liked. He was prudent enough to suspect that there would be protection spells on the Crystal, and he did nothing to thwart his odds at retrieving the Stone. He would wait until the faeries descended from the ship, thinking they were safe, before he attacked. Thus, it came to pass that not one of the faeries realized who he was until the very end when a young faerie child cloaked as a human child chanced upon him while she played hide and seek.

The Dark King had not been faerie for very long, and his concentration level was that of a very young faerie. Because of his deep concentration, he did not hear the little girl curiously walk into the room and watch him. He had conjured up an image of the Stone, and it floated in front of him.

The little girl had been warned that anyone seeking the Crystal was dangerous. Scared now, she rushed up the stairs. In her haste, she dropped the toy she'd been holding, and the loud noise broke the Dark King's concentration. He saw the tiny feet running up the stairs and immediately knew what happened. Without sparing a moment, he ran after her, only to be met by a crowded ship. Everyone was watching as the ship neared land.

The Dark King jostled his way past the crowd to where the faeries were, but it took a long time, longer than it should have, and he smelled the magic in the air. Damn them! He was furious now and tried even harder to get through the crowd.

It was just enough time for the faeries. Quickly, the mother of the little girl tied the pendant around her neck and wove a spell. It was a spell for her to forget everything until a few words were spoken, in which case, she would remember everything. The same was done for the little boy. As they sent the children, who now believed themselves to be human to the deck, the Dark King came upon the parents. The children ran out of sight in the crowd, but the parents had stayed behind to fight. They fought a noble fight, a brave fight, but they were no matches for the wickedness. The Dark King yelled for help from the humans, explaining they were witches.

"Humans have such a fear of witches; it's always seemed silly to us since witches are usually interested in herbs for healing. Witches and faeries, we don't have a lot of contact, but we've always respected them, at least the real ones. Not your pathetic ones who need faerie bones ground in their spells because they can't really do magic."

"Faerie bones?" I ask.

"I'll explain later," she says.

Without questioning the deckhand's accusation, the humans stormed to help, thinking they would be cursed unless the *witches* were killed. The little girl's mother was able to do one last deed before she died. She sent a telepathic vision of what was happening and the spell cast on the children to the faeries who were waiting for them on land.

The children had no idea what was happening and happily walked down the plank once it was set. Because they no longer believed themselves to be faeries, the Dark King could no longer distinguish them from the other human children—a part of the spell the little boy's father had thought up. Frustrated but excited by the violence that had occurred, he hurried away from the docks, thinking the children had already turned back into faeries.

All this, the Dark King thought about while he made plans. He knew the queen would go retrieve the Stone, and once it was in her hands, he knew he would never be able to find it. It was important to get it right away, before she had time to go back to her kingdom. His plan was simple—so simple and perfect. Yes, it was perfect. Today was going to be the day!

"The thing about spells that humans don't understand is that there is no rule book. Each faerie has his or her way of doing them, and it has to come from a certain point of consciousness. Once a faerie has gained the experience, the concentration comes easily, making complicated spells look like nothing more than a wave of the hand."

"Huh." I'm a little taken aback. I thought they just make things happen. I mean, magic is just waving your hand around and muttering, right? Apparently not. Go figure, faeries are not perfect. Well, I could tell you that, believe me. Juniper still hasn't folded her laundry, and now half my bedroom is her stuff, which is mainly comprised of her clothes, both of faerie cloth and uh, you know, regular cloth.

"So, once they and you, I guess, do a spell a few times, it gets easier?" I ask.

I separate my cardigan from her red-and-black-striped stockings.

"More or less. A spell can exhaust a faerie if it's something she is not used to doing, or if it's a big or powerful magic. Our version of school is learning the thousand or so spells that every faerie knows, but then also learning how to create our own. The way I stun someone might not be the way my cousin does."

"So when the Dark King was on that ship, the spell he used to act human wasn't the same as the other faeries'?"

"Probably not. I mean, who knows, but that's why he needed a few hours to try to find a spell that would illuminate the Crystal to him. He knew who had the Crystal, but he also knew, or suspected, that they put protection spells on it. Remember, he never went to faerie school. What takes us minutes took him hours. Honestly? It's all pure speculation. All we know is from the accounts of the children."

As I mull this over, I lose myself in the story. Despite myself, I've gotten interested, though I'll never let Juniper know.

"The Lost Faerie Children—they were Matilda and Robert?"

Juniper doesn't answer; she just smiles and turns up the music.

I look down and realize I've folded all our clothes. All of her blacks, purples, leather, and lace are folded neatly in piles next to my cardigans, jeans, and flannels. Damn faerie! Tricking me into folding her clothes!

Queen Arum was done spying. They were faeries, and they didn't know it. The Crystal was around the girl's neck, the one they called Maggie. She was radiant with the Goodness coming out of the Stone. She could tell that Maggie, Matilda, and Robert could feel something in the air; they were restless. The two families that had been picked to travel across the ocean disguised as humans were from two very important faerie clans. They'd chosen a Warrior family—Dragonbreath—of the Warrior Clan and a Healing family—Wildbrook—of the Healing Clan.

The woman's parents were of the Warrior Clan; she could tell by the green eyes. There was fighting blood in her. The male's parents were of the Healing Clan, the gentleness about him gave that away. The woman's family name would be Dragonbreath, and his would be Wildbrook. And their daughter, Maggie, had a little of both.

Queen Arum tried not to get too excited. The fact that she'd found the Lost Faerie Children was a task that would be told in stories, poems, and songs. So long—a hundred years!—had gone by that she had doubted if she'd ever find it again. Now that she found the Crystal, her fears of having it fall into the Dark King's hands was an even realer threat. They would need to act right away.

"Okay, wait. I don't get this time stuff. You'll have to explain it to me again." I enter the bedroom, notebook in hand.

Juniper is on my bed, reading trashy magazines. "Did you see this dress? They say 'best dress of the year' but it's plain old silk, nothing special about it. That is not the best dress."

I roll my eyes. She's become obsessed with movie stars. Like totally crazy over them. I don't own a television, and I don't buy trashy magazines, but between grocery store checkout lines and the fact that TVs have become a staple in restaurants—which just proves we are all going to become complacent zombies—she's learned all about movie stars.

"Can you put that down and help me with this?" I ask.

She sighs and looks at me like I've ruined her day. "We've been over this already!"

"Just bear with me for a couple of minutes, okay?"

The faerie sits up and stretches. "All right, but let's go get a cup of hot chocolate while we talk."

The street is relatively quiet in the afternoons, and we don't pass many people. The coffee shop is only a few minutes away, and I know I won't get what I want until she's done commenting about everyone's clothes—her favorite topic since she discovered the trash rags and *Project Runway*.

"Can you believe that girl is trying to pull off stripes and plaid? Seriously, she needs a wakeup call."

"That girl is like ten years old!" I say.

"So, her mother should teach her fashion now or that poor girl is going to have a tough time finding a lover," she retorts.

"I think she's acting her age, which is completely appropriate. She's not thinking about lovers yet anyway," I respond, shaking my head. Jesus, I'm starting to think my housemate needs to get laid because lately all she's been talking about is sex. I've even had to kick her out of my bed. Yeah, you're right. She has her bed on the couch so you can imagine I was kinda creeped out to find her snuggled up to me. Snuggled is a nice way of saying … something else.

Anyway, we walk into the coffee shop, its warmth engulfing us, a relief from the stinging cold outside.

He sits at his usual table. I know the faerie sees him because she gives me a sidelong look and a quick smile. "Aren't you going to talk to the boy?" she asks.

"You know I can't."

"When was the last time you tried?" she asks as we wait in line to order.

"I don't know … a few months ago."

"He's looking over here! He's looking at you."

I don't want to turn around, but it's what I do, and sure enough, he's staring at me with a smile.

I turn back to Juniper and shake my head. "So what?"

I fold my arms across my chest to signal the conversation is over, but she has other ideas.

"I have to go to the bathroom." Off she goes, leaving me alone as my crush of two years walks up to me.

"Hi. Charlotte, right?"

I nod, surprised, and give what I hope is a cute little smile.

"I asked Jen your name … don't worry, I'm not a stalker. You can ask her."

I still don't say anything, but I nod my head like a wobbly head doll and wait for him to talk.

"So, you must live around here. I mean, I see you almost everyday, even weekends … I guess you could work around here …"

I don't offer any information.

"Well, I live right around the corner." He points in the opposite direction from where I live.

"I l-l-live o-v-v-ver there." Pointing in my direction. Damn my stutter. I instantly feel stupid.

Luckily, it's my turn to order. Oh wait, not so lucky because I'm stuttering, and he's still standing next to me.

Jen, though, is an angel, "The usual, Charlotte?" she says so I don't have to speak.

I nod, happy she's rescued me.

"And for your friend? Hot chocolate, right?"

Again, I nod, smiling at her. She must have read my eyes because she winks. I look to see if Cutie Pie saw the wink, but he didn't because he's looking at the pastries.   Thank God for small miracles.

I give her the money, and now I'm not sure what to do. I want Cutie Pie to keep talking to me, but I don't want to say anything in case I can't spit it out. Oh, damn, what to do?

Juniper comes out from nowhere, sneaky thing that she is, and sidles up to me.

"Did you tell her to put extra whipping cream?" asked Juniper.

I shake my head.

"Excuse me. Would you mind putting extra whipping cream on my hot chocolate?" she asks.

Jen smiles. "No problem. I should have done it in the first place."

Cutie Pie is done looking at the pastries and is standing awkwardly next to me.

"Don't by shy, Charlotte. Who's your friend?" asks Juniper.

Damn her! "Umm, I, uh, don't know his name." I'm surprised I didn't stutter and feel a little queasy.

Cutie Pie smiles. "I'm Orion."

She smiles expectantly at me, waiting for me to introduce her.

"This is Juniper," I say, thumb in her direction.

Orion smiles. "Hippie parents too? Did you go through the I-want-a-normal-name stage in high school? I wanted to be Nathan."

Juniper looks puzzled. "Why would I want to change my name?"

Orion shrugs uncertainly. "You know, named after a plant—"

"Evergreen actually, and I changed my name *to* Juniper. Orion is much better than Nathan."

Orion looks at me uneasily.

"Don't worry. It's not just you. She's socially inept, and I'm her only friend." I say all this without tripping over my words, and inwardly I am doing cartwheels. I wonder if I'm showing my surprise because Juniper smiles at me.

"Well," she says, "we've got to go. Nice meeting you." And with that, she gently steers me to the door.

Fresh air hits us, and the sky is bright white with the clouds hanging low.

"Fifty years in human time is long." She starts in like nothing back there just happened.

"I didn't stutter once just then. Did you see that?" I ask incredulously, barely walking so that she has to grab my arm and pull me.

"Of course. For a faerie, who can live five hundred years, fifty years is the beginning of life, infancy. So, what you have to make the readers understand is that—"

"No, no, no. You don't understand. I've never been able to speak to him because of my fucking stutter, and today I did!"

"Yes, let's get back to faerie age please. How was it possible that a hundred years could pass and these O'Malleys stay young and vivacious? Firstly, it was their faerie blood; technically, they were young. Lily Brightwater and the family who took Robert in were, as it should be known by now, faeries. They had kept the children home for years, and it wasn't until the children were, like, a hundred and eighty years old in faerie years that they started human school. They looked and acted like human school-aged children and didn't remember anything of the homeschooled years. Those years of homeschooling were purposefully blurred so the children would assimilate with humans better."

I try to wrap my head around all this, and you'd think that living with a faerie for a few weeks would make me believe anything, but the truth is it still confuses me. And I can't stop thinking about the fact that I didn't stutter.

"So, they were young faeries who thought they were human, were homeschooled as faeries, and then went to school as humans?"

"Yes, what's not to understand?"

Ugh. *Everything, you dumb faerie*! I don't say anything because I have a funny feeling she might have helped me speak with Orion, and I don't want her good will toward me to run out.

"By the way, what is a hippie?"

Queen Arum had not been queen when the Crystal had been sent over from the Old World. She'd lived in the palace as a princess, and she could barely remember the commotion it created. Hiding the Stone had been a heavy burden for her father, King Elk Heartsong. When he gave his crown and throne to his only daughter, Arum, he retold all that he knew. The last message Mistress Lily Brightwater sent before living the rest of her life as human was that the children were safe—and they did not know what they had in their possession.

At the time, everyone thought it would be best if it stayed that way, what with the Dark King so nearby. It was thought that eventually King

Elk's faeries would find Lily, Matilda, Robert, and his adopted family, and they would return to faerie realm. After years of searching, they never did find them, and Mistress Lily never once broke her promise to act human for the rest of her life. She didn't even let the queen know when she was dying, so afraid she was of the Dark King.

There was one other piece of the puzzle Queen Arum knew: during their homeschooling, both Matilda and Robert were taught faerie songs, verses, and passages of their history. It had been decided they should know as much as they could learn in the years before joining the human children. It was inevitable that there would be a day when they returned to faerie realm, and they deserved to know of their people.

Before the children started human school, Robert's adopted parents and Matilda's auntie wove a forgetting spell, one that would only be broken with a few words. They were verses from a song every faerie knew and loved. Hopefully, along the way, they'd hear it and remember what they really were. It had been thought long ago—when Arum first became queen—that Mistress Lily had passed on. Mistress Lily was already old when she first took on the task of meeting the Dragonbreath and Wildbrook families at the docks. Neither Queen Arum, nor her father before her, had any idea where Robert and Matilda could possibly be and feared they would be lost forever. There were some that hoped this was true, for the Crystal was safest if lost, but others thought it best to search for it. Then it could be restored to its proper place in Faerie.

Queen Arum did not know of the passing of Robert's family. She assumed they were still in hiding with the children; she still thought of them as children. They were grown with a child of their own, but it was clear in the house there were only the three humans: Robert, Matilda, and Maggie.

The queen was in deep thought as she transformed from spider to faerie. All this time/space matter can be quite confusing to humans, even to faeries who thought they were humans. One did not take kindly to finding out one's true age, especially if the difference was upwards of one hundred and eighty years. She would have to approach this very carefully.

As she flew away from the window crack she'd crawled out of as a spider, a shadow descended on her. The shadow was too large to be a faerie. No, it was an ogre, an ogre that worked for the Dark King, and Queen Arum knew she was in big trouble.

"Tell me what you did with the Stone!" The Dark King was angry. How did she spirit it away so quickly? Damn ogres, all brawn no brain. He should have sent a faerie—no—he should have done it himself!

The queen said not a word, but she stood regally among the filth and slime that crusted the Dark King's palace. She was a beacon of radiance, and her silence was damning.

"For the last time, tell me what you did with it!" He slapped her across the face, but still she did not speak. His breath was rank and hot, and his mouth was so close to her face that spit shot out and landed on her cheek. She would not say a word; she would not break. This was bigger than she herself, and she knew how little she was in the full story. Should she die keeping her secret, should the Dark King ever find out where the Stone was, there was hope for the kingdom she loved so much.

"Take her to the dungeon and lock her in a cell that has no light. See how she does then." With that, he stormed out of the throne room, ready to seriously hurt someone.

The Dark King raged inside. Like the time on the ship the Stone was so close and yet was unattainable. He had to contain himself around the queen; she would be of no use dead. Stomping out of the room in which she was being held captive, the Dark King was looking for a fight; he eyed everyone he passed because someone needed to die. His loyal henchmen shied away from the storming king, knowing the slightest wrong move or word could send them to a painful death.

The Dark King spotted a silly little faerie, someone that worked in the kitchens. He was a weak and sad faerie, perfect for the way the Dark King was feeling. He grabbed the poor being and ignored the weak faerie's cries as he dragged him to the torture chambers.

Phoning my mother is a bittersweet experience. On the one hand, I'm sorry she lives so far away, and I want to crawl through the phone to give her a hug, but on the other hand, living on the moon wouldn't be far enough away from her worrying.

"And the job? Tell me you quit that job," she said.

What she doesn't understand is I'm willing to work a shit job if it means I get time to write. She still doesn't get that I want to be a writer, with a capital W. What the hell did I get an MFA for, after all?

"How's your roommate? Are you getting along? Don't you live in a one bedroom?"

The questions didn't stop, and I regretted calling her. I don't like that feeling, like it's better to not deal with her. Then I think of my dad, and I'm glad I called. Not to talk to him, mind you, but to give some relief to my mother. I really think I might be the product of the mailman, or I got switched in the hospital. The one time I asked my mother, she rolled her eyes. I was serious, but she didn't take it that way; she doesn't treat much somberly, or soberly for that matter, unless it's the social and financial well-being of her children. I was the only one who got the stutter, and although I'm the middle child, I get babied more than Gilly.

I sit feeling drained. I stare at the computer screen, but I don't see the words. I'm just sitting and staring. I don't like writing about the Dark King; he's creepy and ruthless. What I put in the story in no way amounts to what Juniper has told me, but she doesn't want the story to be too heavy.

I've grown fond of these characters, and I'm starting to think that some of them were, or are, real. The way Juniper speaks of the queen and the Dark King. He was into some fucked-up shit, no joke. Juniper went into detail on how he maimed a faerie using a rusty screwdriver. I won't tell you the rest; I had nightmares for the next few nights.

Juniper clearly loves the queen, and I wonder if she knows her personally. Did she know the O'Malleys? Were they real or just made up for the story? I know Wendolyn is real; she describes her so lovingly.

I am broken out of reverie when I hear Billie Holiday turned on. With the rain outside, it is a perfect choice, and I'm glad that my uninvited guest has great appreciation for such things.

Juniper comes in with a mug of strawberries. "I thought you might need some food."

I look down at the strawberries and smile. I would rather a sandwich or better yet a greasy piece of pizza, but strawberries will tide me over for now. "Thanks."

Since the coffee shop incident a few days ago, I've tried to be nice to her, which is, I can tell you, hard. Yesterday, she told me I looked like a lump of unfinished clay, and today, she said it's a wonder I hadn't killed myself because I was so boring. All this after I took her dancing last Thursday! Which was a lot of fun actually.

I'm tempted to go to the coffee shop again today, but I don't want to mess anything up.

"I need a hot chocolate. Let's go," she says.

I guess I don't have a choice.

As we walk the couple of block, I think about asking her if she was responsible for my no-stutter session with Orion, but I don't want to inflate her ego, so I keep silent. You know how tension builds between two people? Like a balloon? Suddenly you wonder how no one else can feel it, and you think the other person has to feel it too because it's crushing you? Instead of bringing that up, I ask about the other thing I've been curious about. "Why do you want all this written down? I mean, why now?"

Juniper looks at me. Her eyes have a way of focusing on you like a tractor beam. They pull you in and don't let go. "It's a gift." That's all she says, and I don't have time to ask more questions because we are at the coffee shop.

A deep breath, and I pull the door open.

I hope I look casual as I look around, and then I hope my disappointment doesn't show on my face because Orion is not there.

Juniper links my arm with hers, a sweet gesture actually, and says softly, "I'm sorry. I hoped he'd be here too."

I look at her then and realize—despite how much she annoys me—I don't hate her anymore.

M aster Spidertamer was worried. That was putting it mildly. He was very, very worried. It'd been a day and a half, and there was no word or sign or instruction from his Majesty.

She was to check in every so often, and the last time she'd checked in was as she was approaching the human house. Master Spidertamer was fond of his queen. Should anything happen to her, he would be devastated.

Master Spidertamer paced up and down his study, hoping his movement would joggle his brain. He'd hate to raise a false alarm. On the other hand, not acting when the queen may be in serious danger seemed wrong.

A knock on the door broke in on his thoughts, and he was glad for the interruption. Perhaps it was good news. The guard let in a faerie he didn't know well and who looked very scared.

"Yes?" Master Spidertamer asked.

"My name is Mister Rain. I oversee the weaving? Well, you see, it might be nothing, but I thought it might be something, so then I thought someone should know," said the faerie.

Master Spidertamer motioned for Mister Rain to sit, and when he did, Master Spidertamer took a seat himself. This did not seem of any kind of importance, and while Master Spidertamer's patience ebbed, he realized the kingdom had to keep running smoothly, even if it meant listening to inane complaints.

"I have a worker, Missy Pine Hollowtree, she is good but slightly daft, yes? And she hadn't shown up for duty. This happened two days in a row, and I was angry, so I went to her chambers, mainly to yell at her. Well, she wasn't there."

"This is hardly something to be worried about, Master Rain." Master Spidertamer tried hard to keep his annoyance from showing. The queen was missing, that was of serious concern, not some worker who was most likely three sheets to the wind, and under someone else's sheets to boot.

Master Rain shook his head in open disagreement with Master Spidertamer. Despite his earlier admission, his body language showed how serious he did believe this to be.

Master Spidertamer looked down to the faerie's hands: one tightly gripped the table while the other tightly gripped itself, making a fist. Master Rain looked to where Master Spidertamer's attention was and waited until Master Spidertamer's eyes were back on his.

"Of course, I thought she had run off for fun, but then when I went looking for a clue as to where she might have gone, I found this." He slowly opened his hand. In that hand was something that had never been seen in the kingdom. It was a piece of bark, a very particular piece of bark. Its red hue was unnatural, not at all like the redwoods but much more red. And it stunk of dead bodies. There was only one place this bark grew: the Forest of Blood Trees that surrounded the Dark King's realm.

Master Spidertamer gingerly took the piece, and as he held it, he could almost hear the screams of the being whose blood had fed this tree. Master Spidertamer's earlier worries came back doubled. "You indeed had cause for alarm, Master Rain. Have you any idea why she would have this?"

Master Rain shook his head. "Missy Pine Hollowtree is flighty, but in the past weeks, she's missed much of her duties. She would claim she'd been working the whole time and that it was a bad joke I was playing on her for pretending she'd missed time."

"Thank you for coming to me. Please go continue your work," replied Master Spidertamer.

The faerie looked relieved to tell someone and believe something would be done; he left in a much better mood than when he'd entered.

Master Spidertamer, however, was much more worried than before Master Rain's visit. A light faerie had been in the Forest of Blood Trees, his queen was missing, and the Dark King was perhaps involved, which meant bad things had been set in motion.

After an hour of agonizing deliberation, he finally decided on what to do. It would be risky for him to leave the palace with no queen, but there was one other faerie the queen confided in, her cousin. Mistress Lantana and the queen had grown up together and were more like sisters than cousins. Master Spidertamer had tutored Queen Arum when she was just Missy Arum, and Missy Lantana would join in just to be with her cousin. Their minds would link in a way few could. It was a gift very rare—even among faeries. If he had to leave the kingdom, he knew Mistress Lantana would do a fine job of keeping everyone from panicking and keeping it running smoothly. He would also send for the faerie that originally found the strange humans. Perhaps she could give him a better idea of these creatures, which would direct him in what to do next.

In just a few minutes, he had Mistress Lantana Heartsong and Missy Wendolyn Brightwing sitting before him. Starting slowly, he pieced together what had happened in the last two days. Ending with the visit from Master Rain, all three faeries looked equally worried.

"Are you sure my cousin didn't just forget? You know how impulsive she can be." Mistress Lantana wanted very much for this to be the case.

Wendoyln was feeling awfully special sitting in this inner circle of confidence. To hear them speak of the queen as impulsive, like she was just another faerie!

"It was my first thought, Mistress Lantana. Too much time has passed, and I cannot find her when I feel for her," said Master Spidertamer.

This deserved a fresh set of worry for the queen's trusted cousin. When a faerie that is tied to another faerie cannot feel him or her, well, it was major cause for concern.

However, Mistress Lantana knew her cousin was not dead. She could still feel the family tug. It was a comfort no matter how small. As long as the family tug kept tugging, they had hope.

"What would you have us do?" asked Mistress Lantana.

"Missy Wendolyn, what was your impression of the humans? Would they have done anything to Queen Arum?" asked Master Spidertamer.

Wendolyn thought and thought. She would be loath to give a wrong answer. "I don't think they would hurt her ... they seemed kind and gentle. There was a sense of magic, and while they were privy to it, they didn't seem to understand it was because of them."

"Do you feel prepared to face the humans, and speak with them?" asked Master Spidertamer.

Wendolyn gaped. What a request! What an adventure! "Yes, I would be prepared for any task you would have me do on behalf of our kingdom."

These were the words Master Spidertamer wanted to hear. He smiled at the faerie and bowed his head to her. "Then it is settled. You have a good feel for these humans and you can lead me to them. In all circumstances, are you prepared to follow my lead?"

"Yes," Wendolyn said.

"Mistress Lantana, the queen trusts you above anyone else. You will take her throne while I, accompanied by Missy Wendolyn, interview the humans. Should anything unusual happen, you contact me without hesitation. Anything at all, and you contact me, understood?"

Mistress Lantana nodded her understanding, awed by her task. She would make her dear cousin proud and keep things peaceful until she came back.

"If someone gets curious, you explain we are on a very secret mission that, once completed, will increase our good fortune," cautioned Master Spidertamer

"Shall I not say we are in search of the Crystal?" asked Mistress Lantana.

"No, do not. There has already been one who was turned to spy on us, one who is currently missing. We don't know if there are more spies ... we don't know much of anything. Should the Dark King know of our actions, well, we would once again live in a strangled fear that he would learn the location of the Stone."

With that, Master Spidertamer and Wendolyn were off. Wendolyn was giddy with excitement. This was something beyond the ordinary, this was extraordinary, and she was thrilled.

"That is very pretty," says Juniper, smiling at me. I'm at my closet, and she has my laptop with her on the bed.

I don't say anything because I'm not used to her being so nice. It's a little creepy actually, like I wonder what comes next.

"You have done a decent job at listening. I am surprised by the sweetness of this piece. She will be very happy with this," continues Juniper.

"Who's she?" I ask. Not for the first time.

Juniper ignores my question. "Don't you have a date to get ready for?"

"You have to come with me, Juniper! I can't meet him by myself!" Getting fully involved with my current situation, knowing whom this book is for comes secondary.

She's convinced me to accept Orion's earlier invitation to a drink at Flannigan's. We had seen him this morning at the coffee shop, and now here I am tearing my wardrobe apart, and trying to convince Juniper, she has to be the third wheel because I don't want to stutter.

She sighs dramatically. "Don't you get it?"

"Get what?"

Her eyes—have I told you about her eyes? She turns and stares at me. I swear I feel like she's reading my soul and finding it to be decayed and black like a cavity on a tooth.

"It's all you, pet. I may have assisted you the first time, but since then, I've had nothing doing."

I think for a second. Actually, I'm paralyzed under those eyes, and I take a moment to say something because I can't seem to move my lips. "I don't believe you."

"I don't care. Besides, I have a date, too."

My astonishment must equal my looking stupid.

"A bloke I met down the street. We're going dancing. It's eighties night at the Moxie!"

Are you surprised a faerie likes to dance to eighties music? I'm not, not anymore.

I pick out a simple outfit, but Juniper puts it back. She picks out something a streetwalker would wear—I didn't even know I owned a skirt that short—and I put it back. Finally we settle on tight jeans and a low-scooped-neck shirt she lets me borrow; God, how I love faerie fabric. It just makes me look awesome. A simple black shirt, and I feel like I could walk a runway.

I try to convince her to break her date and come with me, but before I know it, I'm out the door, wrapped in a shawl I don't remember picking up to keep the cold out, and headed toward the bar.

Flannigan's is crowded, of course. Saturday night. They sometimes have local bands play, and I won't lie, most of them aren't so great.

I see a lot of the regulars at the back counter and smile. This won't be so bad, I tell myself; it's like meeting Orion on my turf. These are my people, and they'll … be watching me.

Oh, shit. Maybe we should have met somewhere more neutral.

Almost getting hit in the head by a guy carrying a cymbal, I forge through the crowd to the bar.

Orion sits with an empty stool next to him. How considerate. I sidle up to him and tap his shoulder. He looks up and smiles. He gets up and kinda straightens his shirt, a white short-sleeved button-down shirt, a la Beatles.

Swoon.

"Hi."

"Hi."

Jesus. This is a bad scene from a movie.

"I saved you a seat." He motions to the stool next to his.

"Thanks," I say, sitting down. Taking off my jacket, I feel beautiful, a rare feeling. For once, I'm not over- or underdressed. I could get used to this kind of confidence. I don't know if it's me, but I don't think its Juniper. I mean, I feel good about me, and it doesn't have anything to do with anyone else. It's strange but revitalizing, like a shampoo commercial or something.

"Ah, my bonny gal! Charlotte, this young'un has been savin' ye a seat," says Donal, the bartender, with a laugh behind his eyes. We are sharing a joke that Orion is not in on.

I smile at the Irish-to-the-teeth barman. "He didn't know," I reply.

Orion looks puzzled. "Know what?"

"Charlotte won a bet. Winner gets tha' spot." He points to the end of the bar where a stool sits empty, right next to where all the whiskeys are neatly lined.

Orion still looks puzzled but doesn't want to seem rude, so he smiles.

My cheeks are a little flushed because it's hot in here and because I'm not sure that the first thing I want Orion to know about me is that I like to accept fun and crazy bets. "It was a silly thing. No big deal. But sometimes we make bets, and the winner gets to sit there. Kinda stupid, but fun," I say.

Donal is not used to my non-stuttering self. Juniper and I came in a week ago, after a long while of not coming in at all. He and all the regulars kept making me repeat words I used to have a hard time saying. It was nice to have them so honest about it. Like at work? They try to pretend nothing's changed, which makes the whole thing damn awkward. And now my mom won't quit with the now-you-can-find-someone-decent. Because I guess people with stutters can't get nice dates?

"What'll you have then?" Donal asks.

Orion looks at me, to let me order first. Really? How nice. I wonder if I should order something girly? Nah. "Jameson on the rocks and a beer back."

Orion again looks at me, impressed like. "I like me a girl that likes whiskey," he says and orders the same. There is a playfulness in his eyes that reminds me of an imp or a leprechaun. Not that I know what one looks like, but now that I have a faerie living in my apartment, I can assure you I believe they exist and that they probably have the same smile behind their eyes that Orion has right now. Well, good. I like me a man with a wild streak and a sense of humor.

Hours go by, and the band sucks, but we've been talking the whole time. I barely tune into the lame-o wannabe rock 'n' roll.

We are both drunk. Knowing the bartender is a blessing and a curse.

The immediate joke is how my death will involve tiny toys that get stuffed into Easter eggs and Christmas stockings.

"No, no, no!" I protest, laughing. "You would not believe how much money people spend on junk. I have no hope for humanity when I leave work."

"What does give you hope?" Orion asks.

I think for a moment. "My sister Joan? She's a teacher. She tells me funny stories, like when one kid dressed up as a flower for Halloween, right? Then this other, littler kid, dressed as a bee, started circling the flower, because that's what bees do, right? And there was something in that story, just picturing a chubby little kindergartener circling my sister's third-grade student. That gives me hope."

We sit for a moment, looking at our drinks. Great. Now that I can talk normally, I realize it's a natural talent that I can stop a conversation in one breath. It wasn't always my stutter. "What about you?" I take a swig of my beer.

Orion looks toward the band and then at me. "Not this band, that's for sure."

And we start laughing again.

Orion excuses himself, and heads back toward the bathroom, a little unsteady on his feet. I try not to fall off my stool.

Despite it being so busy, Donal has made time to lean in and trade good-natured barbs.

"Where's that spicy roommate of yours?" Donal is trying not to sound too interested.

I shrug my shoulders. "On a date, I think."

He looks slightly disappointed.

"She's a bag of crazy. I feel bad for any guy she dates," I say to make him feel better.

"She doesn't come in as much as she used to now that she's shacked up witcha." He says this as if it's my fault.

"What? She came in here before that night?" I ask. I always thought she'd chanced upon that damn poker game.

"All the time, funny you ne'er saw her. She asked about ya. Seems she had ya in her sights as roomie for a while."

Well, I'll be a rat's ass. "And did you tell her I was a writer?"

"I s'pose it came up."

Uh-huh.

Orion weaves his way back to his stool, and the conversation turns away from my otherworldly roommate/trickster/friend. While I continue to laugh and have fun, the idea that Juniper specifically targeted me is in the back of my mind, tugging.

The queen lay in her cell. Never had she experienced such pain—or displayed such strength. She would not tell of the strange unhuman family, of the necklace they possessed. Let them kill her first. The Pendant was too important. It was more important than her life, and she knew that.

Wincing, she tried to get up. She nearly let a cry escape as her arm buckled from under her. She lay back down. From deep in her mind, she could feel a tug, a tug she hadn't felt for a long time. It was the gentle presence of her cousin, and suddenly there was a little bit of vigor in her soul. Sensing her cousin meant that Mistress Lantana knew she was missing, which meant Master Spidertamer had a plan. Knowing this in and of itself was enough to keep her holding on, and with Mistress

Lantana sending her a bit of her own strength, the queen felt almost whole.

Three times the Dark King had sent for her, and three times he failed to get anything from her, despite what physical pain he brought her. That had to be a testimony to her resilience. The queen smiled through the tears that ran down her face. Her body hurt, and she was too weak to weave any mending spells. The one thing she'd been able to do while she bounced in the big ogre's sack was weave a binding spell that would not let any revealing spell open her mouth without her wanting it. No matter what the Dark King did to her physically or with magic, he would not be able to get any information out of her unless he broke that spell. She had bested that horrible human turned faerie, and with that thought, she found dreamland and a little bit of peace.

The O'Malleys went about their business as usual. Maggie begged her mother not to put the necklace back in the attic and keep it on her mother's vanity. Until dinner was ready, Maggie wandered around the house until she ended up in her parents' room again, where she would stare at the necklace and stroke it, feeling tingles up and down her spine every time she touched it.

The O'Malleys had no idea a queen was missing and that the Dark King was making plans, and that all of this surrounded the necklace, which was in their possession.

At the moment, they were eating dinner. Maggie drank juice out of a wine glass. She felt very sophisticated holding the delicate stem. Her parents found her solemnity sweet.

They were startled to hear a knock at the door, and Robert took a minute to get up from his chair, Maggie happily following him. She loved company, and unexpected company was even more fun. As she neared the door, the strange tingles went up and down her spine, the same that she felt in the tent, the same she felt when touching the necklace. A little frightened at this, she stepped nearer to her father, wondering if he felt the same tingles. The fact that he stopped sharply, cocked his head to the side, and took a moment before opening the door told Maggie that her father had felt the tingles too.

Two strangers stood on the doorstep; one was a tall, lean man with a thin face and a long ponytail. He wore an old coat with tails that were striped and completely out of date.

"I'm afraid we've come at a bad time, but our task is so important that we must forgo civility," began this stranger on his doorstep. "Let me introduce myself. I am Master Spidertamer, and this is Missy Wendolyn Brightwing."

The pair made an odd couple. The man appeared to be old, though Maggie would be hard-pressed to put an age to him because he looked so fit and nimble. Maggie turned her attention to the man's partner, a striking woman. Her figure was slight but strong, and her long hair curled around her shoulders. Her eyes were intensely purple, making Maggie wonder if she'd ever seen purple eyes before. She was much younger than her partner, although Maggie would not be able to guess her age either. They were dressed in clothes one might see in a costume shop, and they lived in their clothes as if the material itched and scratched, though made from fine silk. It seemed as if they were time travelers because the clothes were quite out of date.

"We are here looking for someone we've lost. Perhaps there was a woman who visited you earlier in the day? Anything you can tell us would further our search," said the man.

Maggie looked to her father, suddenly interested in the mystery.

Robert looked down at his daughter and raised his eyebrow.

Maggie shook her head.

"I'm sorry, but nobody's come around today," replied Robert.

The pair looked at each other; worry clouded their faces.

Robert sensed their urgency, and because they looked harmless, Robert opened the door wider. "Why don't you come in? We're in the middle of dinner, but we'll take a minute to talk with you."

Master Spidertamer and Wendolyn entered with profuse thanks.

Matilda met them in the living room, surprised to feel that same tingling she had felt in the tent and with the necklace.

"It seems they've lost a friend, and they had the peculiar idea she'd visited us today," said Robert.

"We've been home all day, and no one's stopped by. Maggie, did someone stop by and you didn't tell us?"

"No, no one," said Maggie, not taking her eyes off the strangers.

They were not lying, Master Spidertamer could tell. He could also feel the magic. These humans were not in fact human, not at all. They were faeries, and though he wasn't the best at reading intentions, he could tell they were honest and kind. They would not have harmed the queen; Missy Wendolyn was right. Queen Arum, if she'd been here, would have also felt it. Master Spidertamer was sure the queen would not have taken any action before speaking with him; at least, he hoped she wouldn't have.

"What you are about to hear may be fantastic, perhaps unimaginable, but very true," said Master Spidertamer.

The queen had proven herself a formidable opponent; most would break at this kind of torture. The Dark King sat in his throne.

Unlike the queen, there was nothing regal about him. One leg was thrown over an arm as he slouched back. A platter of sugar confections and sweet pastries sat at his elbow, hardly touched.

Yes, the queen was stronger than he'd thought. The Dark King would have to resort to physical violence now, though he tried to hold himself back. He had to remind himself to go slowly; he could not kill her until he knew where to find the Stone. How he couldn't wait to get his hands on that Crystal. Once that was gone for good, nothing would be able to stop him. All faeries would be forced to recognize him as king! He would no longer sit on the edge of the realm like a leftover thought, like an embarrassment. No, he would be ruler of all, and he would kill those who opposed him.

The queen will be first, he thought.

He'd started with the simple whip—to loosen her up, so to speak. He did not expect her to talk, but he enjoyed the sound of it hitting the queen's bare skin. There are tortures that are physical, and there are those that are emotional and mental. He knew the latter would be more effective on the queen but enjoyed so much the physical aspect of pain that he continued to test her body in various ways. He could also place fire to her wings, an especially excruciating pain for faeries. Once he got bored with that, he could begin the emotional onslaught once again.

As he ate his confections, the Dark King thought about his next move. Would he explain in detail what he'd do to her loved ones? He didn't know if she had family … or maybe he would round up all the faerie children and eat them. Children always seemed to break people; maybe he would start with that. He continued to eat, licking the icing off his long, gross fingers, a smile on his evil face.

Orion has taken me to a small, informal, family-owned Thai place. We haven't ordered yet, just sipped our water. There are cloth napkins on the table, and I wonder why I register that. This is the kind of place where the bill will be more than anticipated, but worth it. I can tell by the smells that come from the kitchen, which are making my mouth water.

I'm not nervous. I actually feel very comfortable with myself, something I haven't ever felt. I haven't stuttered once, and I'm convinced Juniper put some kind of spell on me, no matter what she tells me.

I look across the table and realize that maybe Orion is kind of nervous. I want to laugh but don't. Suddenly he's not the untouchable cute guy in the coffee shop; he's real flesh and blood sitting across from me. This fresh take on him doesn't lessen my crush. It makes it stronger. There is awkwardness about us. The whole built-up, first-real-date thing, and I realize I'm not hungry or thirsty. I don't want to go through the motions of this date, of getting to know him or anything.

"Let's go?" I say, and he looks surprised.

"We haven't … do you not like this place?"

"I like it just fine and want to come back, maybe even tomorrow. But right now, I want you to kiss me, and I don't want you to do it in the middle of a restaurant. So let's go."

Not asking for more details, he grabs my hand, and off we go.

It is well past midnight when I creep into my apartment. I'm high, like that crazy-fun-I-just-spent-the-best-night-with-the-best-guy-kind of high. As a pure hater of romantic comedies, I feel like I'm living one, and I giggle.

The light flashes on, and there Juniper stands with her arms crossed. "Well, I was wondering when you'd roll in."

I giggle. I hate giggling. What the hell is wrong with me?

"I just had the best night!" I twirl, yes, twirl, to Juniper and grab her hands.

Holy shit. Who is this person? Is it really me?

"What in the name of all that is holy is wrong with you?" she says, voicing my same thoughts.

"C'mon, let's dance." I keep hold of one of her hands and press play with my other hand. James's hit "Laid" starts, and I'm glad Juniper, for once, did not put the CD away.

Happiness is infectious, and it really doesn't take much to start spontaneous dance parties with Juniper, so there we are in my living room, dancing our hearts out.

The song ends and we plop on the couch, heaving.

"So you finally got some ass," Juniper says, flaunting her contemporary vocabulary. Next thing you know, she'll be saying things like *vacay* and *realsies*.

I look at her and squint. "Really? I'm in love, and all you can think about is sex?"

Juniper rolls her eyes. "What is love without a little sex?"

"We didn't Do It," I admit, my foot tapping along to the next song.

"What?" Juniper is surprised.

"Nope. We just ... we had fun. He's real funny, and we ended up talking and talking and laughing. We drifted to sleep on his couch, listening to Cat Power."

"Then why are you here? Having awoken me up at …" she squints at the clock, "four thirty in the morning?"

I shrug. "I woke up and then he did and then it could have gotten, you know, X-rated, and I didn't want it to. Not yet, so I left."

Juniper shakes her head. "Shit. You are crazy."

"Says the faerie in my living room." I close my eyes as she begins to lecture me about how I'm the abnormal one in the room, and I let her words wash over me. I'm happy, and I won't let her ruin it.

Matilda and Robert sat quietly while Maggie triumphantly smiled. She knew there was something different about her family. She knew faeries were real—no matter what bratty Suzy said! She stared at Missy Wendolyn Brightwing, who took an instant liking to the girl. A smile from the faerie was like a beam from the sun, and Maggie glowed in Wendolyn's attention.

Her parents, on the other hand, were unsure about what the hell was going on. Yes, they'd felt different. Yes, these past few days in particular. Yes, they were from Ireland. Yes, they came over when they were young. Yes, Matilda's mother had given her a necklace with an unusual pendant. Yes, it was strange this man they'd never met knew all this! But adults didn't believe in faeries; they believed crazy people and children believed in faeries, but rational, sane adults did not. Robert and Matilda liked to believe they were both rational and sane.

"There is a rumor that when the spell was cast for you to forget your faerie blood, words spoken out loud would restore your memory. I wonder now if I spoke some words you wouldn't find it too intrusive."

"Listen, Mr. ... Spidertamer? We are happy to answer your questions, but you do have to understand that right now I'm tempted to call the police." The only thing that was keeping Robert from calling the police was the absence of threat; these two really seemed perfectly harmless.

"Please, I only have a few more questions, and then Missy Wendolyn and I will leave you. Please," said Master Spidertamer, anxiety in his eyes. He knew he only had a short while to convince these humans about who they were, and so far, he'd gotten nowhere.

"Daddy, please! They're telling the truth! I'm sure they are. Please. I know you feel the tingles. I know you do! Listen, okay?" Maggie pleaded with her father. Maggie had gotten used to the tingling going up and down her spine. She'd studied every aspect of Wendolyn and knew like green was green, up was up, and round was round, that this lovely lady standing in her dining room was in fact a faerie.

Maggie watched as her parents read each other's expressions. She'd seen them communicate this way her whole life; they knew each other so well they didn't even have to speak, just stare. After a moment, it seemed they'd come to an agreement, and Robert gave Master Spidertamer a short nod. They either were stalkers, nuts, or something else, but violent did not fit them. Plus he could not ignore the ever-present electricity running up and down his spine. So Robert and Matilda O'Malley continued to hear the stranger out.

"Do the names Mistress Holly and Master Elm Dragonbone mean anything to you?" asked Master Spidertamer.

They shook their heads.

"They were the names of your parents, Matilda. Robert, your parents were Mistress Osmunda and Master Willow Wildbrook."

Robert, with a skeptical look, shook his head. He couldn't keep a little laugh from escaping.

Maggie shot him a look. "Daddy!"

"I'm sorry! It's just so fantastic. I can't … I'm sorry. Those names mean nothing." Robert composed himself as best he could.

Matilda and Robert looked expectantly to Master Spidertamer. He took a deep breath. This was not going well. "Mistress Lily Brightwater was not your blood aunt, but rather the faerie sent to pick you and your parents up. Unable to take the boy in as well, she found a family for you, Robert. Was there ever a song Mistress Lily would sing to you, Matilda? Likewise, was there a song your adopted mother sang to you?"

Matilda thought about her aunt for a moment, it was strange that this man knew the name of her auntie. It was all too bizarre, and she just accepted it; otherwise, she might think it was she who was mad. "There was one song she sung, something about the trees that sway to the music … I forget the rest."

Robert's eyes lit up. "I remember that! It goes, 'The trees that sway to the music know our hearts' content, for they that dance with us from faeries have been sent.'"

Master Spidertamer's heart flipped. Any shred of doubt was cleared away; they really were the lost children! But if the queen had not talked to them, where was she?

"That song is called 'Earth's Secret.' It is our oldest—"

Master Spidertamer stopped talking; right before him, a transformation was taking place. Not of size or shape, but of memory and thought.

Robert and Matilda were remembering who they really were, and while this was an internal sort of transformation, it held the same amount of magic, and the room was still and pregnant. Maggie was not afraid, but she was a little bit anxious as she watched her parents. Though she couldn't see anything, she knew something was happening, and she knew it was important. She edged close to Missy Wendolyn, and the faerie put her arm around her. It was an instant comfort, and Maggie's heart slowed to a normal level of thumping.

Robert and Matilda looked at each other, their eyes wide with belief. It had all come back to them: their lives before, their families, the voyage, and the spells.

Matilda cried silently for the death of her parents, as did Robert, and he held onto his wife. Maggie, never one to be left out, joined in the circle, and the other two faeries had the decency to fix themselves some tea while the family mourned.

The Dark King was angry. The queen was not talking and, worse, not screaming or showing any signs of pain. He had to conclude that she did not have the Stone, and if she did not have it, then the humans must still possess it.

Damn ogres!

He looked up when he heard heavy footsteps approach, and the stupid ogre stood in front of him.

"Masta call me?"

"When you picked up the queen, did you do so after she left the house? What I mean is, did you see her enter, then exit the human dwelling?" The Dark King did everything he could to not explode.

The ogre thought a moment. "Pretty faerie near house, me grab. No in, no out, next to."

Damn him! The Dark King's rage pulsed in his veins. With barely a thought, he used a strength spell to grab the ogre and fling him across the room.

The ogre yelped. "Masta! Me sorry, me sorry," cried the poor dumb beast.

"Be gone."

The ogre limped out of the throne room as fast as he could.

The Dark King snapped his fingers, and three of his trusted guards appeared. "You leave now," was all he said, and without question, they followed him out of the palace.

Matilda entered the kitchen where Master Spidertamer and Missy Wendolyn were drinking their tea and talking in hushed voices. "Thank you," she said to the old faerie.

"I'm sorry about your family," Master Spidertamer said.

Missy Wendolyn comforted Matilda with a hug, and when her arms enclosed around her, Matilda felt instantly peaceful. She smiled gratefully at the faerie.

Maggie and Robert entered the kitchen. Her excitement was uncontainable; she literally had to keep moving or else she thought she would burst. Maggie had the necklace in her hands and gave it to Master Spidertamer.

He took it with apprehension. It was beautiful. So much good in one place was amazing and inspiring.

"We must hasten now, my new friends. Our queen has been missing for far too long, and the Stone needs to be placed in its Sacred Holding Place."

Robert cleared his throat.

"And that's it? You will all be safe?"

"I don't want you to leave!" said Maggie. After searching for faeries her whole life, here they finally were. And for them to leave after such a short time did not seem fair at all to Maggie.

Missy Wendolyn, for the first time, spoke up. "Master Spidertamer, if we found these humans easily, the Dark King might be right behind us. We can't leave them here unattended."

Maggie looked from one grown-up to another. She'd never been in danger before, and the look on her mother's face was not reassuring.

Master Spidertamer looked at the family. Missy Wendolyn was right. The O'Malleys would have to go back to their kingdom with them.

Master Spidertamer clasped the necklace around Maggie's neck. If there were Dark faeries around, they would go after Missy Wendolyn or himself—not after the family, or at least he hoped. "I'll trust this around your neck, little miss."

Maggie smiled at him. "You bet, Mister, I mean, Master Spidertamer." She stood still while Master Spidertamer wove a cloaking spell. Seconds later, no one could see the necklace that still hung around her neck.

"Quick. We will turn you to your natural state, that is, your faerie selves. It will be disorienting, but stick close, and we will reach our realm soon." With that, he and Missy Wendolyn wove spells over the family, muttering words unheard by humans under their breath. Maggie stared at them with such concentration that one would have thought she was trying to memorize the words.

Being transformed didn't feel like anything, which disappointed Maggie until she noticed she wasn't more than six or seven inches tall, and that her hair had turned a bright brick red color. Her mother had that same flaming hair, and her father's stayed a rich black. Their wings were translucent and long—not short and stubby like the cutesy faeries Maggie thought were too sickly sweet.

"We need to get to the vortex, the entrance to Faerie. It is not far, but we need to exercise caution," said Master Spidertamer as they left the house and entered the garden.

Maggie was thrilled to see the flowers loom so large over her. The grass was up to her waist, and the butterflies were the size of large birds. Surely this is what Alice had felt like in her wonderland!

As they zigzagged around redwoods and through wildflower fields, Master Spidertamer kept an eye and ear out for anyone following them. For as vigilant as he was, he did not see that there were indeed Dark faeries watching them from afar.

The Dark faeries had been instructed to go to the house where the queen had been captured and keep an eye on the supposed human family that lived there. Any activity was to be reported straight away, and should they see the Stone, make no hesitation in grabbing it—no matter the cost.

The little band of Dark faeries seemed unsure of what to do at first. Their king had said nothing of the humans turning into faeries or leaving their house. Sending a message might take too long, so they decided to act quickly. Without words, the leader of the pack instructed the others to form a circle around the group and to attack all at once. A simple, swift ambush, and they would have the family in captivity.

They descended on the group of Light faeries, but they were not prepared for Master Spidertamer or his viciousness. Despite the surprise of an attack, both Master Spidertamer and Missy Wendolyn were ready to fight.

Maggie stayed close to her parents, who followed the fighting like sports spectators. Rooted, they watched with horror as the Dark faeries lashed out with their bodies and spells. Fists and rocks flew through the air; bodies were knocked down and jumped back up, ready to fight again.

Maggie, the weight of the necklace on her chest, hid behind her parents.

Missy Wendolyn did her best to keep the Dark faeries from getting too close to the girl, but it was all in vain. As a Stunning Spell sideswiped her, she saw a Dark faerie bind the girl up with faerie rope and sling her over his shoulder.

Robert and Matilda were faring no better; they were also getting roped by a couple of Dark faeries. Master Spidertamer was busy with three faeries himself. She could do nothing but watch them fly away with precious Maggie and her parents.

As soon as the fighting faeries saw their comrades had captured the family, they stopped fighting and instantly followed the others. Master Spidertamer sat on a rock, wheezing with fatigue. He'd put up a good fight, but three faeries to one are bad odds, and he was lucky to get away alive.

When he saw that Missy Wendolyn was stunned, he undid the spell. It took a little while; these Dark faeries were thorough.

"They are traveling slower than normal with the weight of the O'Malleys," said Master Spidertamer. "Go follow them, but keep your distance. Do not try to fight them. If you can make contact with the O'Malleys, let them know I have gone for help."

Missy Wendolyn nodded, a little frightened. "I will leave marks to guide you, and I shall tie myself to you so that I may know when you are near."

Master Spidertamer nodded and smiled. Tying selves through magic was a good way to feel the presence of another, to know that allies were still alive, to warn of danger. This was an old, but useful, war tactic.

"The little girl, she'll be all right, won't she?" Wendolyn was worried.

"The Cloaking Spell should hide the Stone," said Master Spidertamer, unable to comfort Wendolyn.

Missy Wendolyn turned herself invisible but made sure to keep the Dark faeries in her sights. It was a good thing that Missy Ronwen Moonbeam insisted that they learn invisibility spells when they were younger; they used to get into so much trouble. Well, look at her now, using it to help track the Dark King's henchmen. Missy Ronwen would be proud.

A few times, one of the Dark faeries would look back, probably sensing faerie magic, but not seeing anything, would press on, flying faster and faster.

Missy Wendolyn cloaked herself in another spell, and she made herself smell like the redwoods they were flying in and out of. *Ha, take that, Dark faeries!*

The Forest of Blood Trees is well known in Faerie as a place to avoid. The legend goes that the Dark King, angry the Stone got away, immediately set forth before him a path so grim with murder that the trees learned how to live off the blood. Through the roots, these trees hungrily sucked on the earth rich in blood, growing into rusty red, tangled masses.

It is said that in the course of a year, many beings must die in order to provide sustenance for the trees. The ground stays moist with the blood of the unfortunate beings that dare anger the Dark King.

Missy Wendolyn Brightwing flew in the forest, among the trees, her fright growing as she passed the trees. The smell of rot stung her nostrils so strongly that she nearly fainted. Down below, she saw scavengers eating at the fresh carcasses. Out of the many, she could only recognize the forms of two or three bodies. A large one provided nourishment to a family of rats. It once had been an ogre but now was a pulpy, meaty mess. Two smaller bodies had been faeries; she could tell by the glow in the skeletons. In the distance, she spotted a goblin collecting the glowing bones. *He'll get a good price for them on the black market,* she thought. Faerie bones were widely known to enhance any spell, and rudimentary witches were fond of their use.

Missy Wendolyn kept on, and though she couldn't see the Dark King's henchmen, she knew she was on the right path.

The forest got thicker and thicker still; the trees were darker than before and older, much older.

The wind had little room to pass as the leaves of the trees created a ceiling. A sort of hushed wail whispered as if the trees sang the laments of the fallen.

Finally, in a small clearing stood the oldest, most twisted and rotting tree among them. She had reached the Dark King's castle.

While Wendolyn followed the Dark faeries, Master Spidertamer was flying faster than a firefly. As soon as he reached the palace, he blew on the emergency horn. He heard the instant rustling of wings as all the warriors heeded the call. The horn had not been blown for a long time; he would have to tell them something.

Mistress Lantana was proving herself to be very efficient and knew just what to say. Together, they would energize the kingdom and get the warriors ready for battle.

The cell was cramped with the three O'Malleys and the queen. When Maggie awoke, she saw her parents rubbing their eyes. They all must have had some sleeping spell put on them.

Matilda and Robert immediately hugged Maggie, and rather annoyingly insisted on checking her all over for any scrapes or scratches. It wasn't until they were done fussing that they saw the queen, unconscious in the corner.

Disentangling herself from her loving parents, Maggie went over to the hurt faerie, deeply concerned. Matilda followed; the sight of Queen Arum took her breath away.

"This is the queen; it must be. She looks hurt, tortured," Robert exclaimed.

Maggie stroked the faerie's face, and Queen Arum opened her eyes. "I've … humans, you are …" and she went back into her sleep.

Maggie cradled the faerie's head in her lap and placed her hands on her beautiful head. Within her fingers, she could feel tingles, like little bits of electricity sparking around the faerie's head. She could feel things moving within the faerie's head. Astonished, she took her hands away. If she had to put a word to it, she'd call it the faerie's magic, or essence, that she'd felt moving around. Was Maggie doing the right thing? Maggie began to radiate a little; white light poured from her pores.

Robert could see a hint of uncertainty in his daughter, and without knowing why, but knowing it was the right thing to do, he leaned over to give Maggie a kiss. That kiss created a spark that traveled all the way through Maggie's hands. That kiss produced a glow within Maggie, and the glow was showing her what to do.

Maggie stopped paying attention to what her parents were doing. She put her hands back on the faerie's head, and with her magic, she began to go deeper and deeper into the faerie, sensing just where she was hurt.

Robert took off his jacket and put it over the queen. Matilda began rubbing the queen's arms and hands to keep them warm. They watched as their daughter began to focus on what she was doing. Although they didn't know what was going on, they knew it was right. There was something in the air, a sort of zing, and it was a good zing. They stayed out of Maggie's way and continued to keep the injured queen warm.

F or any human, the sight would have been extraordinary; it would even take a faerie's breath away. Hundreds of warrior faeries flew in formation with Master Spidertamer in the lead. He tracked the clues left by Missy Wendolyn, grateful for her cunning.

They finally came upon the Forest of Blood Trees. The sound of hundreds of wings made the bone-collecting goblin look up. So imposing was the army that he quickly scurried away. Master Spidertamer looked down at the blood-soaked earth that fed the trees. He felt sick to his stomach. All Light faeries had heard the stories, but none (expect for poor enchanted Pine Hollowtree) had seen it.

Soon they came upon the Dark King's castle. It was sick from the inside, perfect for the Dark faeries to reside. Master Spidertamer stopped; the magic was oppressive. The warriors stopped behind him, making not a sound. Their wings were quieter than the sigh of a baby, which was impressive since there were hundreds of them.

Missy Wendolyn was huddled on a branch close to the sad, dying tree. She'd seen where they'd taken the family, but she couldn't get to them because a magic spell guarded the perimeter, and she was having a hard time breaking it.

In her quiet concentration, she felt Master Spidertamer's presence, and flew to the front of the tree. He was there with the army of the queen, and what an army it was! She looked on with awe at the strong, tense bodies of the strongest male and female warriors, prepared to die protecting their realm.

Missy Wendolyn flew down to speak with Master Spidertamer, a smile on her face. This may have been the most dangerous day in her life, but she wouldn't have traded it for the world.

Master Spidertamer listened to what Missy Wendolyn said. Another faerie's perimeter spell was hard to break, but if they could find the faerie that cast it, they could reverse it. How, though, would they find the faerie?

"The spell is not unbreakable. I almost have its undoing. If you can cause a diversion, it may be enough to break the concentration of the faerie producing it," said Wendolyn.

Master Spidertamer thought about this. They could not enter the palace until this spell was broken, and surely the Dark King knew of their presence by now. If he were smart, he'd have set up alarms to alert his guards to trespassers, alarms they'd surely tripped. His failure to acknowledge them meant that he had confidence in the perimeter spell.

"Appeal to his ego. Challenge him. His army will have to come out here. The Dark King would not risk lifting the perimeter spell lest you storm the castle," continued Wendolyn.

Master Spidertamer nodded, acknowledging the intelligence of the plan. "You are not afraid, Missy Wendolyn? To witness battle is not an easy thing to forget."

"I must help. You will need to focus on the strategy of fighting. I will undo the perimeter spell. It is the least I can do for our queen, for the little girl."

Master Spidertamer smiled, and Wendolyn knew she had made a friend for life in Master Spidertamer.

When he saw Wendolyn find a safe hiding place as close to the fortress as she could, Master Spidertamer looked over the warriors. They all looked strong, they were all willing to fight, and they were all willing to die. To Master Spidertamer, that was even braver.

The Dark King was on his way to speak with the prisoners. The tunnels in the rotted tree that served as his palace were dark and gloomy. He quickly followed the winding path until he got to the chamber of prisoners.

He saw the girl cradling the queen's head. It looked like she had healing powers, and this made him angry. What imbecile put them all in the same cell?

"Stop it. Stop it, you little ingrate!" he spit out. The Dark King hated children!

Maggie looked up, frightened. The girl's father moved in front of her to protect her. The mother stood. No fear was visible on her face. This angered the Dark King even more. He called to the guards who stood in the room. "Which of you idiots put them all in the same cell?"

The guards did not answer; they looked down at their boots, worried they might get hurt.

"Grab that little girl and put her in her own cell away from the queen. The other two will have their own cells too, and while you're at it, put the father in the torture chamber. He needs a little roughing up." The Dark King gave this last order with a wicked smile.

The mother stood in front of her husband. "You will not take him or my daughter." Her voice was low and even.

"Matilda, don't make it worse!" Robert pleaded. Why was his wife so unafraid?

"Robert, our daughter has found a gift, and I know I was meant for something else. Trust me?"

Before she could say anything more, the guards unlocked the gate and advanced toward her. She knew now why she was so good at athletics, why her muscles ached to be stretched and used. They tingled with the anticipation of a good fight, and she crouched low, ready to spring like a lioness. Robert too got into position; they would not take his daughter from him.

Maggie knew the best thing she could do was to stay with the queen. Concentrating with all her might, she blocked out what was happening and focused on the task at hand. If the queen could heal enough to lead, then maybe they'd have a chance of getting out.

Had Maggie looked up, she would have seen her mother fight like a demon and her father like a tiger. It became clear that Matilda had warrior blood in her, and she was giving them all she had. The Dark King watched this with amusement in his eyes; he loved battle, he loved violence, and he loved the sight of blood. Robert was breaking away from his captors, but they reeled him back in.

Matilda snarled like a wolf and threw a guard against the gate. While faeries love their magic, they are hesitant to use it in battle. Too much could go wrong, and their concentration is limited. This was an advantage to the O'Malleys, who were keeping the guards at bay.

While they fought, the Dark King stood aside and tried to sense the magic around him, trying to sense which one of them had the Stone. One of them had to be carrying it; where else would it be? But he could not feel it, no matter how hard he tried.

Suddenly, in the middle of all this carnage, a noise rang loud. It was Master Spidertamer's horn, and the Dark King heard it. He knew there was an army waiting for his own. They had tripped many magical alerts as they marched toward his castle.

Those stupid Light faeries challenging him! The Dark King would answer to the challenge, slay his foe, and come back to kill this family that had inconvenienced him so.   To the first guard, he gave orders. "When you have separated them, call for me. I've changed my mind about the father. Take the girl to the torture rooms instead." He turned, ready to face the challenge. His guards would soon be able to overtake the faerie-humans in the cell and soon he would be king.

The Dark King's exit from the castle was impressive. His army flanked on either side, oozing from the large gates like an infection. He addressed Master Spidertamer. "Tell me," said the Dark King after his army had fallen into place, after the clanking of armor had stopped, after the quiet before impending battle fell like the ash of a volcano over them all. "What will you do when your queen is dead? I shall very much need an advisor to help me run the whole of Faerie. I hear you do well by her; perhaps you would do the same for me?"

"I would rather die," answered Master Spidertamer calmly, his face showing no emotion.

The Dark King shrugged. "Well, then, I will make sure that happens. Slowly and painfully so that you may remember I offered you an alternative."

The Dark King grinned; he would have fun killing this faithful friend to the queen; maybe he would have her watch. Oh, it was great fun being the Dark King!

There was no start, there was no warning shot, and there was no ready-set-go. Both sides waited, growing more and more impatient, letting the tension build and build and build until in unison arms were raised, battle cries were issued, and armies lunged. It was not a dance, and there was no grace. It was kill or be killed; it was bloody and ugly and horrifying. It was bodies slashed in two; it was guts spilling as the clanging of swords muffled anguished cries. It was war and death, and nothing more can be said.

Missy Wendolyn almost had it; she could feel the spell bending. She just needed a little longer, and she'd be able to enter the castle. She could hear the battle cries, the death cries, the sound of armor and weapons. Shaking her head to free herself of these noises, she turned to her important task and continued altering her spells, certain she could find the right one to unlock the guarding spell.

Sure enough, she felt it break, and with her heart singing, she flew to where Master Spidertamer could see her. He looked up, and she waved, letting him know she'd succeeded. Even from where she was, she could see him smile and nod his thanks. Without waiting any longer, she flew around the back of the palace to find a way to sneak in.

At the back palace gates, Missy Wendolyn was determining her possibilities. There were only two guards, and they looked bored. The Dark King hadn't prepared for his perimeter spell to break, the foolishness of overconfidence.

Missy Wendolyn remembered a trick she and Missy Ronwen did once to their parents. They'd made a noise ball in order for the grown-ups to look the other way. Filling the ball with funny sounds, they bound it with two spells, one making the shape of a ball, and the other making it fly. While the parents looked in the direction of the noisy spherical distraction, she and Missy Ronwen stole away with a canister of wine, later making themselves sick on it. Smiling at her childhood shenanigans, Missy Wendolyn went to work. It was tricky without a second pair of hands, but soon she had a ball filled with screams and shrieks. Missy Wendolyn let it fly past the guards, high above their heads. It would have distracted anyone to hear such bloodcurdling screams, and luckily, both guards went after it, leaving the gate wide open to her.

She flew through quickly and abruptly came to a hallway with many passages. Which way? She closed her eyes and sent her feelers out. Down. She had to go down; she could feel the little girl below her. Without wasting time, she turned left and found a staircase leading down. She followed the stairs until she reached the first landing. She heard voices and quickly hid behind a twisted root. The guards went running past her. The warriors were making good headway with the front gates. She waited until she could no longer hear their footsteps, and then she continued down the staircases.

Missy Wendolyn found the dungeons—dark, dank, and smelly. Mold grew in the rotting roots of the tree that served as the Dark King's palace. There were guards ahead of her; she could hear them. Walking softly, she prepared a stunning spell. She could only hit one with it, and she'd have to act fast. Slowly, she rounded the corner.

Immediately, a guard spotted her. "You, stay where you are!"

As the guard advanced, she hit him with her spell. The other guards would have responded, but they had their hands full with putting the prisoners in separate cells.

Matilda took the opportunity of the distraction to kick her warden hard in the knee. The guard let out a howl and slapped her across the face.

Robert hit his guard in the nose, and soon another brawl was in full force.

Missy Wendolyn dodged the guard coming at her and hit him with the stun spell. She liked that spell, very handy these days. She continued to look for Maggie. She glimpsed a guard going down a corridor with the girl. Maggie was struggling as hard as she could. The guard kept his grip on her, but just barely.

Good girl, thought Missy Wendolyn. *Keep it up. I'm coming for you!*

Missy Wendolyn skirted the fighting to try to get to Maggie. As she swung into a dungeon cell to avoid Matilda and a guard, she looked down and saw her queen, alone and unconscious. She paused for one horrific moment.

A guard saw her transfixed and hit her hard on the head.

Rage filled Missy Wendolyn's throbbing head. The sight of the poor girl being captured, the sight of her queen lying desolate, and the sight of the O'Malleys fighting to help save her kingdom were just too much for her.

Had the guard known how angry she was, he might not have hit her. Like a wild banshee, she went for the guard's throat and ripped out his vocal chords. Her loud battle cries after this ghastly act were enough to make the others stop. Up until then, no one had been in this fight to kill, just to overpower. The guards were following orders, and the O'Malleys were just trying to get away. They all, the Dark and Light faeries, stood so still in a silence that it seemed as if the stun spell had been brought upon them. The smell of fresh blood in the air changed everything, and suddenly everyone knew this fight was to the death.

Matilda spared no time and yanked her opponent's head hard to the left. He sagged with his head lolling unnaturally to the side.

Robert unsheathed the first guard's sword just in time to block a blow from another guard.

Missy Wendolyn rushed down the corridor where Maggie had disappeared. She knew that if she didn't save the girl, this fighting was all for naught.

Master Spidertamer continued to fight out in front. Sending some warriors to the back of the castle, he hoped Missy Wendolyn had been able to get in and find the O'Malley family. They were almost through the front gate, but it would still take a while.

Looking behind him, he saw one of their bravest and finest warriors fall. It happened so quickly; the faerie had been so young. Violent death was not easy to witness; he was doubly saddened he'd died following Master Spidertamer's orders. There was no time to mourn the young faerie though; he had to get inside.

A loud cheering made him turn around, and he saw that they'd broken down the gate. Master Spidertamer watched as the Dark King flew up and over the front gate, disappearing from sight, clearly headed to a secret entrance. Master Spidertamer shouted some direction and then sped off to try to find the Dark King.

The Dark King raced down the corridors to get to the dungeons. There was mayhem everywhere. The O'Malleys were formidable fighters, and four of the five guards were dead. He rushed down to the corridor that led to the torture chamber, and he found the girl tied up, struggling to undo the rope that bound her. A Light faerie was fighting one of his guards, and while they were distracted, he scooped up the little girl and headed for his chambers.

Maggie let out a scream that pierced his ears. Hitting her across the face, he did not slow his pace. She whimpered for a moment and then let out a howl like she was a wolf. Again he hit her, but again, it did not stop her. A third time she screamed, and this time, she let out a name. "Queen Arum, wake up now!"

The mention of the queen's name angered the Dark King, and this time, he hit her so hard that she fell into unconsciousness.

Back in the dungeons, the queen sat up, awake and full of energy. She felt the call of the young girl. She stood up and saw the fighting. The door to the dungeon was still open, and quickly she slipped out. Without hesitation, she sent spells flying into the guards. They dropped to the floor, instantly asleep.

The O'Malleys looked behind them and saw the queen smiling at them.

"Quickly this way." The queen could feel Maggie's presence.

They rushed down the hallway, Matilda and Robert's hearts racing wildly. If anything happened to their little girl, anything at all ... it was better not to think about it.

They got to the torture room just in time to see Wendolyn fall under the strength of the guard. Quickly Matilda attacked him from behind, and down he went. She hit true and fast; the poor guard didn't have a chance.

Wendolyn stood up, weary but happy. She bowed low to the queen, but this was the only bit of formality she showed. "Quickly, they went through there," said Wendolyn, pointing to the corridor on the left.

Taking the lead, the queen went first, followed by the O'Malleys and Missy Wendolyn.

The palace was a maze of corridors and hallways. Master Spidertamer issued orders for the warriors to spilt into groups and take different corridors. He sat still for a moment; he was still tied to Wendolyn, and now he could feel the presence of the queen. They were together somewhere above him. They were moving.

Trusting the warriors to do their job, he chose a hallway he thought would lead to the queen, Wendolyn, the O'Malley family, or all of the above.

They were lost. The O'Malleys were starting to panic. What if they were too late? Hallway after hallway they ran, but there was no sign of their daughter.

The queen stopped suddenly in the middle of what felt like the hundredth hallway. She closed her eyes and reached out her hand. "She's in there."

"But there is no door!" protested Matilda.

"He has hidden the entrance; most likely this is his personal chamber."

Missy Wendolyn immediately began to weave location spells. Robert began pounding on the walls. He knew it was no use, but he had to do something—and he didn't know magic. Matilda joined in, and together, they began to call her name.

The queen helped Wendolyn find the right spell to uncover the door, and this is how Master Spidertamer came upon them. He heard the pounding and followed its uneven thumping. As he rounded the corner, the queen and Wendolyn were performing acts of magic.

With a cry of joy, he ran over to his queen, breaking her concentration. She smiled at her advisor and told him what they were looking for. He grew grave; he knew how hard it was to undo another faerie's spell. He, too, joined in. The three faeries stood in utter concentration while Robert and Matilda kept calling her name.

M aggie awoke on a floor of cold stone. The Dark King was standing over her, sneering.

She could hear the faint cries of her parents; they weren't too far away! She sat up, and the Dark King pushed her down. She was very frightened, more frightened than she'd ever been. What stood above her was pure evil, the kind of evil that paralyzes and preys on anger, fear, and weakness.

The walls around them began to shift, and the Dark King looked up, worried. He looked back at the girl and snarled. "Where is the Crystal?"

"I ... I don't know."

The Dark King hit her. The sting was strong enough to bring tears to Maggie's eyes; afraid, she kept her head down.

"Where is it?" he demanded.

Maggie knew her parents were close. She had to give them time to find her. Looking straight into his horrible eyes, she said, "I don't know."

The walls began to shake again, and Maggie knew that was good.

The Dark King looked almost afraid. He grabbed her and spat into her face. "I will kill your parents in front of you, slowly so you can hear their cries over and over. I will take each and every finger from your tiny hands and feed them to trolls. Do you understand? Now tell me where the Crystal is!"

Maggie suddenly had an idea, and she prayed it was the right thing to do. Using her real tears of fright, with her voice shaking, she said, "It has a hiding spell on it. It's around my mother's neck." *Please, don't let any harm come to my mother.* Maggie wondered if she was right to trick the king. If he found out what she was doing, she'd surely die a horrible, painful death.

The Dark King laughed and pushed her aside like a piece of garbage.

What the king did not know was that behind the walls to his chamber were the queen, Master Spidertamer, and Wendolyn. He underestimated the powers he was about to face. Thinking he was in control and beyond harm, he undid his spell that hid the door to find Matilda, kill her, and take the Stone.

Instead, in came the queen, Wendolyn, and Master Spidertamer. Right behind them, ready to fight, came Maggie's parents. The queen had a paralyzing spell at the ready, Wendolyn had a mummifying spell, and Master Spidertamer had a sleeping spell.

All three hit the Dark King, sending his ugly body into contortions, writhing on the ground. They were too many spells at once, and no faerie, no matter how powerful his or her magic is, can take that kind of abuse. Seizing up and then bending in pain, the body made noises as bones broke.

Robert and Matilda ran past the fallen body to Maggie, who was still on the floor crying. She hugged her parents, not letting go for a second. The three sat on the floor watching the Dark King's body writhe with pain. His screams were deafening, and Maggie covered her ears. The queen, Wendolyn, and Master Spidertamer looked on as if they were made of marble. For so long, they had lived in fear of this monster, and now he was dying. It was not relief they felt—but shock.

The whole thing was over. Had it been days or minutes? It felt like both all at the same time and everyone was drained. The O'Malleys sat on the floor, unable to move. The queen, her advisor, and Wendolyn wrapped the Dark King in a shroud. He didn't deserve it, but they didn't feel right taking him outside uncovered. The O'Malleys watched the faeries, their mortality close to their thoughts and the last screams of the Dark King still in their ears.

It would be too easy to say that no one else had died, that the fighting ended as soon as the Dark King was killed, but war is never clean and simple. It wasn't until the queen and Master Spidertamer exited the palace with the Dark King's body that the warriors, Light and Dark, realized it was over. Even then, there were those so faithful to the Dark King that they kept fighting, trying to kill as many of the Light faeries as they could before dying themselves. As far as wars go, this was a quick one, unlike the one between the faeries of the East and the goblins of the North. That had lasted for decades and had left many families to bury their sons and daughters.

Life is nothing less than a gift. The mystery of death haunts our curiosity. The sheer number of corpses a war leaves behind for some is exactly that: a number of victory or defeat. For those who are left to bury, mourn, and honor the fallen, their loved ones are not numbers but pieces of their hearts. The conquering heroes wear their victory like shields. They fight to protect and win. The deaths of their comrades are sad but noble ends to brave lives. Do the mothers of the fallen think that as well?

The procession was amazing to behold: the warriors, tired but elated by their victory, and the queen in front, regal, majestic, and properly somber. The warrior faeries followed their queen back to their kingdom, the dead carried in front with great reverence. The fallen would be given spectacular burials with celebrations lasting for days. These heroes who sacrificed their lives would forever be honored in song, verse, and memory. Faeries do not easily forget the pain of war and the cost of life. They do not revere the bloodshed, but despite that, they are fiercely proud of their warriors.

The warriors who survived returned home to be nursed by their families and friends, and the O'Malleys were given a special apartment within the palace. The queen's handmaidens and valets doted upon them, giving them food they'd never tasted or even thought existed: apples from trees that fed off of rose petals or guavas ripened by the light of the moon. They drank juices from honeysuckle vines and wore lavish robes that felt like air and seemed to change colors as they moved.

Maggie made friends quickly, which never happened in her human state. After being fed marvelous delights like pure sunbeam yogurt, she would run off and play, climb trees, study bugs, and laugh.

Robert and Matilda felt like royalty, their spirits finally mending after all the cruelty they had witnessed. They listened to old stories and songs, remembering some from their first childhood with their parents, and some from their second, when they were homeschooled. Distant relatives told of their parents, stories of them growing up, getting married, of even Robert and Matilda as children and how they had always had a special bond. Matilda and Robert's parents had been close friends and had hoped one day their children would bind both families into one. It made their distant relatives happy to see that it had become true—and to see they had found their way back to Faerie.

After three days and three nights of festivities, it was time to go. The three of them longed for their home, and while they were among their people, they wanted time to adjust and say good-bye to their old lives slowly.

The queen sent them home with gifts of fine cloth, handmade jewelry, and faerie gold. They left in the company of their two very good friends, Missy Wendolyn Brightwing and Master Spidertamer, and as they walked the palace steps, every faerie stood, cheered, and waved to their friends who helped save Faerie. The attention was humbling, and Maggie, Matilda, and Robert stood for a moment looking at all the faeries, all the friendly faces, and all the big smiles cloaked in the finest of clothes.

That the O'Malleys never quite went back to normal life was to be expected. Maggie was not able to adjust back to being human. If before she'd felt different, now she knew it, and she made no effort to become a part of any crowd.

Robert and Matilda weren't quite as ready to leave their human lives, and they sent Maggie to live with Wendolyn. They would visit often. After a while, when Robert and Matilda's lack of aging was becoming obvious, they decided to cast off their human lives for good. Without packing more than a suitcase of photographs and books, they said good-bye to the old house and everything in it, leaving the neighborhood children to make rumors and ghost stories about what had happened to the family.

The day they returned to Faerie for good was a happy day among faeries, and so it's been told, the celebration for the return of the family who helped bring down the Dark King was no less than thirty-two days. It's been said that party has yet to be topped.

"**I**s it true?" I ask.

Juniper looks at me. "Yes, the party lasted thirty-two days. I told you, we party."

"I mean, this story, did it really all happen this way?"

The faerie looks at me with a quiet sort of sadness. "Yes."

I watch as the printer keeps spitting out page after page.

"Queen Arum, hailed to be one of our best, was succeeded by another wonderful and powerful queen, one whom I still serve," said Juniper.

"You ... you know Queen Arum? I mean you were alive?" This surprises me. I don't know why, but I've had a nagging feeling this whole time.

She laughs. "Of course, silly. We live a long time, remember?"

Suddenly it hits me; it all comes clear. She didn't grow up among her kind, she read human books, and she changed her name.

"Maggie?"

Juniper smiles.

"You're Maggie, aren't you?"

She nods.

"Who's your queen now? Who was this for? Is someone dying? You act like someone is dying!" All of this comes rushing out of me, and I feel upset. I don't want anyone to die, not any of these people—beings, whatever they are—I've gotten close to them. I've gotten close to her, to Juniper, and I don't want her to be sad.

Juniper, who is really Maggie, sighs.

"Queen Arum stepped down fifty years ago due to a sickness. The torture the Dark King invoked on her had a spell that gave her a slow sickness. Mistress Lantana took her place, with Mistress Wendolyn as an advisor. I too am an advisor, but I've always found time to spend with Arum. She is close to the end now."

"This is for her, isn't it?"

"Yes."

"Why me?" I ask.

Juniper shrugs. "I'm allowed my secrets."

"Seriously?" I hate secrets.

"If I told you everything, there wouldn't be a reason for me to visit again, would there?" she says with a sly smile. Ugh, cunning little thing that she is.

The printer stops, and there, on the last page, reads the title with my name under it, as told by Juniper.

"I have to change the title," I say.

"What will you name it?" she asks.

"The Faerie Tale of Maggie O'Malley?"

"Sounds stupid."

Oh, boy, and here I was getting all goopy.

She left in the middle of the night. On my kitchen table is a small pouch and a bundle of clothes she left for me. The pouch is full of gold coins and a small note: *Because I tricked you.* And under the clothes is a mix tape, songs we listened to together, songs that were the backdrop to our bickering, to our conversations.

Well, I guess she's not all bad after all.

A month ago, I would have said she was a scourge on my life, invading it like a Roman army, and now that she is gone, the apartment is empty. I was lonely before she came, even if I didn't realize it, and now it comes creeping back.

But there is a change in me as well. I feel inspired, and I suddenly know what I want to write about. What might have been muddled ideas swimming, circling each other, are now clear and in focus. My thirst for music is almost tangible, and it becomes clear that my novel will involve music, magic, and myself.

She'll come back to visit—I know she will—and I am content to start my novel with her mix tape playing, inspiring me.

About the Author

After spending seventeen years in theater and acting out other people's stories, Carmen decided to put her own words on paper. Classes, workshops, and seven years of writing lent to many forms of storytelling—from short plays to screenplays and now to fiction. Having found her strength in fantasy/faerie tales, Carmen is ready to share her first novella.

Carmen lives with her husband, two kids, one cat, and eight chickens in a small town on the Central Coast of California. When she is not writing, you can find her playing her ukulele, gardening, or starting one of her multiple art projects.

About the Book

Charlotte's tidy and simple life gets turned on its side when she loses a poker game to Juniper, a faerie. Juniper gets to move in with Charlotte while Charlotte writes out a story Juniper tells her: a story of the faerie Queen Arum, the Dark King, a magic crystal, and the O'Malley family, who find themselves in the middle of a battle between good and evil. Charlotte's now chaotic life forces her to stretch her limits both socially and emotionally, and she finds that maybe she needs a little excitement after all.